THUN[DER]
STORM

BOOK II

Joe Medina

SILVER BULLET

ENTERPRISE SYSTEMS

Joe Medina's Library

joemedina68@hotmail.com

bulletjoemedina@gmail.com

www.joemedinaslibrary.com

Phone: 1-323-231-6613

Joe Medina's books are solely available on Amazon.com

Published by SILVER BULLET ENTERPRISE SYSTEMS 07/03/2019

ISBN 13: 978-1077462731

Any images depicted are private property of © Silver Bullet Graphic Solutions and are used solely for illustrative purposes.

The concepts expressed in this work herein are solely the views of the author and do not necessarily reflect the views of the publisher, and the publisher hereby disclaims any responsibility for them.

TABLE OF CONTENTS

ECAPTION

Lezama is a time traveler trying to get to home. His ship has been compromised but is trying to drop in on 3550 A.D. into a society that has the technology needed to repair the time capsule.

Unfortunately society has enslaved itself and is kept from encroaching technology of Lezama's time capsule. He can't land in the required time frame and keeps bouncing off the High Commands frequency shields. He needs a homing signal.

Using the technology of the time capsule, Lezama transmits his thoughts into physical bytes to his descendants, piggy backing such signals within the transmissions of the High Command.

Janno is an athlete who answers the call. Luna is an engineer who also answers the call. All around the academy students are heeding the call, the call to Thunder Storm an underground hidden society that revolts against the System with freedom being the prize and death the answer of the High Command to those who would rebel.

Lezama disguises himself as a Counselor as he communicates with Janno on what is needed to land his ship in the correct time frame in order to save the children who have been genetically engineered by the High Command. Humanity has evolved.

Thunder Storm is split into two groups: students and cadets but work as one to escape the wrath of the High Command's system control enforcers; the Sentinels.

Janno was abducted by a Sentinel and taken to a medical facility where his identity has been erased and replaced by another personality. The Counselor, Lezama has disappeared having been shot by a laser in the astral plane a plane that the High Command has discovered through geometric formulas.

Thunder Storm has escaped the Beaumont Campus. The High Command has destroyed over eight thousand people to preserve its function. Janno in his new personality has been assigned to a Janitorial division of a cleanup crew at Beta Six. His first glimpse of the outer system is dead bodies he's been ordered to dispose. And in the midst of the chaos, there is hope.

𝒯HUNDER STORM: PART TWO

CHAPTER EIGHTEEN
SECTION ONE: CLEAN UP CREWS

"𝒜lright ya dirty bunch `o swine!", yelled the Superintendent, "Get off yer butts `n on yer feet! Now!!"

"Huh? Wha?"

"Whassamatter der, Rook?! Ya need a special invitation ta' join da' rest `o us?!" Rook was a short term word used in place of "rookie" in the Janitorial Field of the System.

"Huh? Uh? No" Janno answered.

"No, what?! No, What?!" hollered the Superintendent in Janno's face.

9

"No Sir!" Janno responded.

"Freakin' Rooks tink dey can cum' in heah `n start disrespecting der superiors?!" yelled the Superintendent, "Well der freakin' wrong?! Am ah right?! Dangitt, Ah asked if Ah was right?!"

"Yes, Sir!" yelled out the Clean-Up Crew.

"Ah can't freakin' heah you!!"

"Yes, Sir!!!" re-hollered the team. There was a chuckle among the ranks.

"Dangitt Ruffer?!" called out the Super intendant, "Ya' tink dis is funny?!"

"Uh? No Sir!" Ruffer answered.

"What?!"

"No Sir!!" Ruffer repeated.

"Well Ah tink you're bullstuffin' me, servant!!" yelled the Superintendent, "Drop `n lemme heah ya count `em out loud."

Ruffer dropped to the floor and began executing "push-ups", an on the spot disciplinary action used on disruptive servants among the Janitorial Ranks of the System.

"Alpha One!" Ruffer yelled, "Alpha Two!" There was another snicker among the ranks. The angered Superintendent marched to the source.

"Ya' tink dis is a joke?!" he hollered, "Wipe dat smirk off yer face, Gormely!"

"Yes, Sir!" Gormely said.

"What?!" asked the Superintendent, "Did Ah ask fo' an answer?!"

"Uh? No. Sir!" responded Gormely.

"What are ya answering fo', then?! Shaddup n' drop!!!" came the hollering order. Gormely fell to the floor to join Ruffer. The Superintendent had become enraged. "Screw it!!" he yelled, "Everybody drop!!!"

The Janitorial Division from Society Unit Beta 3 had been assigned Clean-Up Detail. The amount of work was overwhelming. It was necessary to enlist the aid of Institute Assigned Janitorial Personnel. It was given to them the task of clearing the blackened fields, left behind by the slaughter by Sentinels, the Society Units ordered destroyed at

Council Call 215. Institute Assigned Janitorial Personnel were divided into crews. The crews naturally were identified by numbers and letters. Clean-Up Crew Beta One was currently undergoing discipline for the unprofessional manner in which they responded to duty.

The team yelled out, in sequence, the repetitional push-up executed, "Alpha One! Alpha Two! Alpha Three!" And in the midst of the counting:

"What's with him?" Janno asked Allen, "Alpha Four!"

"Who? The boss?" Allen identified, "Alpha Five! Oh, don't worry about him. He's just cranky at this time of the day, Alpha Six! It's been said a piece of shrapnel got caught in his head, Alpha Seven! And caused interference during his Initialization Sequence, Alpha Eight! It's why he talks the way he does, Alpha Niner!"

"Really?" Janno whispered in amazement, "Alpha One Zero!"

"Nah! I'm just kidding" Allen confessed, "Beta One! He's an acehole just like the rest of them, Beta Two! It's their nature. He used to be a Sentinel."

"Oh?" Janno remarked, "Beta Three!"

"Razz?" Allen asked, "Beta Four! You really are a Rook, aren't you? Beta Five!"

"Uh? Yes, I guess I am" Janno answered, "Beta Six!"

"What's your name?" Allen asked, "Beta Seven!"

"My name is John" Janno answered, "Beta Eight!"

"Where do you come from John?" Allen asked, "Beta Niner!"

"Unit Delta Six", Janno answered, "Beta One Zero!"

"Hmm?" Allen pondered, "There's a lot of bad rumors going around about that place, Gamma One!"

"Huh?" Janno asked, "What do you mean? Gamma Two!"

"They're planning to delete the unit" Allen answered, "Gamma Three! You're lucky you got out when you did, Gamma Four!"

CHAPTER EIGHTEEN: SECTION TWO
PRISONER TRANSPORT

And at the High Command Central Core Chamber: <Unit Delta 6 Digit One to Central Core Unit Digit One: Digit One holds Delta 6 prisoners in custody. Elements: awaiting interrogation process. Request Central Core Chamber entry, over!>

<Unit Delta 6 Digit One, this is Central Core Chamber Digit One, transport elements to chamber Alpha Six; access code @#^. Sentinel entry at chamber Alpha Two; entry access code @#@. Prepare for decon procedure. Digit One acknowledge>

<Central Core Chamber Digit One, Delta 6 Digit One acknowledged. Digit One out!>

CHAPTER EIGHTEEN: SECTION THREE
SECTOR CHI 7, QUADRANT 4

Sector Chi 7, Quadrant 4 was the Systems Automatic Recycling Center. It was here where scrap metals and re-usable matter were stored. One of the Center's unique identifying marks was that it was kept unmonitored as was the rest of the Outer System. "Listen!" Yuan announced, "We're slowing down, the air brakes!"

"I think we've reached the dump sites" Ace expressed.

"Warriors?!" Peff called out, "Standby! Thunder Storm: stand alert!" Everyone in the truck prepared to disembark.

"How is she?" Jeppe asked.

"She'll recover" Nette answered, "Thanks to your stasis

field we were able to shove her shoulder back into its proper place without inflicting pain. Her wounds have been treated. It's just a matter of time before she comes to."

"I take it she can be moved then" Jeppe assumed.

"Yes, but very carefully" Nette agreed.

"Thank you" Jeppe said. He donned his helmet on and picked Luna up in his armored arms.

"Standby people!" Peff called out, "The doors are sliding open."

"Hey?!" Yuan expressed, "That's not all. The truck is being tilted. We'll be crushed by the weight of the garbage!"

"Everybody out! Move it" Peff hollered. Arco and Orge motioned for the truck's sliding door and quickened its opening. They helped the others clear out. Astian, Arlos, and Yuan were the first ones to exit. Seeing the exterior environment of the truck to be filled with more garbage, they scurrilously climbed over the dumps helping other members to Thunder Storm flee the crushing weight of the falling out garbage.

"Let's go! Let's go!" Arco yelled, "Move it out or your dead!"

"You're great for encouragement!" Orge remarked.

"Why, thank you" Arco responded.

"Ok, you two, clear out!" Peff ordered, "Everyone's safe."

Arco and Orge moved away from the truck's falling debris. Orge climbed to join the others, but Arco tripped and jammed his foot in muck. The garbage hovered above him and for a split moment Arco sensed his end. "Aw shoot!" he said. And the garbage dropped.

CHAPTER EIGHTEEN
SECTION FOUR: TRIAL BY COUNCIL

And at the Central Core Chamber: The prisoners entered the Alpha Six Chamber to undergo decontamination process. The Decon Process was new at the Core Chamber. It was installed to keep the MDV virus out from the High Command's network. Delta 6 Digit One entered the Alpha Two Chamber. It proceeded forth to the Central Core Communication Chamber to monitor the events back at Delta 6 keeping track of the unit's sentinel division.

The prisoners were escorted in one by one to meet the awaiting Prime Dean at the receiving hallway to extract individual performance records for the court to review. He was to plead their case individually. The prisoners were kept apart from the Central Core Chamber to await their respective trials. Cheynne was revived and set on his feet. His body had reverted to normal and he was clothed. Jeena wanted to go to him but was kept back by the Core Chamber's guarding Sentinel. Out in the vast hallway, she could hear the thunderous voice of the High Command. She shook with fear.

<The court will systemize itself!> came the order, <Let the prisoner come forth!> Dean Joan

was led into a spacious hall. All was silent. Only the padded sound of armored boot complimented the scuffle of prisoners in digital chains. Then; <Commence!> the High Command ordered.

<High Command Case Delta Six Alpha One!> announced the Central Core Chamber Digit One, <Dean Joan Ojahn Three versus the System, in effect!>

<Case Review?> demanded the High Command.

<Dean to Beaumont Campus: Third Stage Institute at Society Unit Delta Six> Reported the Prime Dean. <Campus Status: under quarantine. Selected Fit Personnel failed to report for Breeding Assignments. Terrorist Acts against the System in effect. Campus Dean found in violation of

Charter Alpha Six: Section One, Beta Clause: Failure to Maintain Order within Educational Institutes. Council requests minor discipline: previous misconduct, non existent. Request for Assimilation and Re-assignment filed>

<Requests: under system analysis> said the High Command, < The Defendant will now speak!> Dean Joan was shocked. She had never been at a High Command Review Board. She never dreamed of nearing the High Command Central Core Chamber much less be allowed to speak before it. But where was the High Command himself? She could not see him. Only the Council sat around before her and the Prime Dean at her rear. The wide spacious hall was silent as the Court was waiting to hear Dean Joan's defense. She was awed.

{Assimilation and re-assignment?}, she thought, (It's more than I had hoped for. I will maintain my Dean status and be kept alive. Oh, Troy?! If only you could have been here, I would not hurt so....} She dropped her head and tears formed around her eyes. And as she answered, she felt she was betraying Troy and his dream. "No Contest!" she announced.

<Dean Joan Ojahn Three> spoke the High Command, <You are hereby found guilty of failing to maintain order within the Third Stage Educational Institute at Society Unit Delta Six; Violating Charter Alpha Six; Section One; Beta Clause. You are hereby sentenced to report to Unit Sigma 5 for Assimilation and Re-assignment. Case Delta Six Alpha One end input file!> Dean Joan was led away to await escort and transport to Unit Sigma 5 so that

her sentence could be carried out. Jeena stood within the prisoner's detention cell. She was frightened. She heard it all.

<Let the prisoner come forth!> came the command. Cheynne was led out to face the Court. Jeena called out to him. But he did not listen. She began to cry. <Commence!> ordered the High Command.

<High Command Case Delta Six Alpha Two in effect!> announced the Central Core Chamber Digit One, <Cheynne Ojahn One One versus the System!>

<Case Review!> came the order.

<Medical Assistant Instructor Cheynne Ojahn One One> identified the Prime Dean, <Code

C 3-A Element at Beaumont Campus; Third Stage Unit Delta Six. Element Charge One; Violation of Population Control Act; Beta Clause, Section 4.5; Failure to report for Breeding Procedure.

Charge Two: Element: in violation of the Oath Charter; Delta Amendment, Section 6.2; Willful Participation of Terrorists Activity.

Charge Three; Element: in violation of Uniform Dress Code; Gamma Clause Section 3; Indecent Exposure. Record reviews indicate no previous misconduct. Code C Element suspected to be carrier of MDV virus. Decon Process indicate no virus found.

Element: hazardous to the system. MDV virus: in dormant status. Appeals: non existent>

<The Defendant will now speak!> ordered the High Command.

"I am Cheynne, a human being!" he announced wasting no time. "I hereby declare myself a free man, subservient to no one but the Most High! You who calls itself the High Command are a thing of naught compared to He! Wherefore this trial is a mockery of Justice! As a free man, I shall breed and mate with whom and when I want, for this decision is mine to make and not for anyone, but the Most High, to order. I do not participate in Acts of Terrorism for I have never lifted up my hands in violence against any man nor machine, unless it was for the preservation of life, freedom, and the Most High!

And as for being nude in public, I was born naked and

naked shall I die! For dust I am and unto dust shall I return yet in my flesh shall I see my God! And whence I return unto my flesh I will stick my foot so deep in your rear console my boot print will be burnt onto your screen for eternities to come!"

The sound of silence filled the court room. In the prisoners holding tank, Stick shift had dropped to his knees at hearing Cheynne's declaration and prayed to the Most High. {Oh! Father!} he thought, {Forgive me my unworthiness and grant that I may come unto you quickly, for I am in fear of life. And though I shall die, grant that I die with faith in you, in the name of the Most High, do I beg!}

Jeena was stunned at Cheynne's speech for never had she heard any member of Thunder

Storm proclaim their beliefs with such courage and in the face of death. <Execute the will of the System!> ordered the High Command. Thick metal doors slid shut to cordon off the prisoners holding cell from the court hall. Similar doors slid open above Cheynne exposing the nucleus of the System. The High Command's power source was a nuclear generator emitting high level radiation lethal to un-initialized personnel.

The Initialization Sequence performed on the Elite was not only to control their function but to protect them from the powerful frequency waves, at their peak, at the source. Cheynne's brain was fried. And from where she stood, Jeena could hear his cries. "No! No!" she yelled, "They're killing him! They're killing him, Cheynne!" But she could do nothing. Cheynne had not been the first to die in this manner. Others were capture while fleeing annihilation from Society Units ordered destroyed by the High Command at council call 215. They too had been put to death.

<Let the prisoner come forth!> ordered the High Command. Stick Shift was led out from the holding tank. Jeena reached for him but a Sentinel held her back. "Do not worry, my dear friend" Stick shift said to her, "It is not death where I go to, but to freedom I embrace!" Jeena's tears came in waves.

<Commence!> ordered the High Command.

<High Command Case Delta Six Alpha Three, in effect!> said the Central Core Chamber Digit

One, <Stick Shift Ojahn Two Eight versus the System!>

<Case Review!> came the order.

<Stick Shift Ojahn Two Eight> identified the Prime Dean, <Code C 6-A Element at Beaumont Campus; Third Stage Unit Delta Six. Element Charge One; Violation of Population Control Act; Beta Clause, Section 4.5; Failure to report for Breeding Procedure.

Charge Two; Element: in violation of the Oath Charter; Delta Amendment, Section 6.2; Willful Participation of Terrorists Activity.

Record reviews indicate no previous misconduct. Appeals: nonexistent>

<The Defendant will now speak!> ordered the High Command.

{Father, grant me strength that I not falter} Stick Shift thought to himself. And he was filled with courage. "I am called Stick Shift" he began, "I am a philosopher who values life beyond price. There is nothing more precious in existence than life itself. And yet every action has an equal and opposite reaction. This is part of relativity concepts. And where there is life, there too lies death. But death is a thing of naught for it is a temporary thing. And its opposition being life is everything, for it is everlasting to those who come unto the Most High. Being a thing of value, it is not forgiven to shed innocent blood. I declare to you that whatever actions you cause to come into existence, shall come to take full effect upon you. This is law of thermodynamics. Wherefore I die an innocent man, retribution shall befall you and the law of thermodynamics shall be fulfilled in compliance with the axiom of relativity, for you shall be destroyed, and may you rot in hell or in your case, the junk yard!"

<Execute the will of the System!> ordered the High Command. And Stick Shift's horrid screams ripped across the hallway. Jeena shut her eyes tight. She was next. Cheynne and Stick Shift had died martyrs.

{Change!}, she thought, {Change! Dangitt! It's not working!}. Jeena was hoping to metamorphose that she may escape. She had no way of knowing how the change came about, for she was not at the Recovery Ward when Cheynne had explained it to their junior companions. Jeena, of course, fit qualifications for the metamorphosis, but her time had not yet come.

<Let the Prisoner Come forth!> she heard the order spoken. And Jeena was led out into the vast hallway opening.

<Commence!> ordered the High Command.

<High Command Case Delta Six Alpha Four, in effect!> announced the Digit One, <Jeena Ojahn Six versus the System!>

<Case Review!> came the order.

<Jeena Ojahn Six;> identified the Prime Dean, <Code C 3-B Element at Beaumont Campus; Third Stage Unit Delta Six.

Element Charge One; Violation of Population Control Act; Beta Clause, Section 4.5; Failure to report for Breeding Procedure. No previous misconduct files detected. Counselor Request: minor discipline. Request element: return to carry out Breeding Assignment>

<Request: under system analysis> said the High Command, <The Defendant will now speak!>

"I'm not breeding with anyone!" Jeena hollered, "I'd rather die!"

<Jeena Ojahn Six> spoke the High Command, <You are hereby found guilty and in violation of Population Control Act; Beta Clause, Section 4.5; Failure to report for Breeding Procedure. It is the will of the High Command that

you are returned to carry out Breeding Assignment! Case Delta Six Alpha Four end input file!>

"What?!" Jeena protested, "No way! No way!" But her protest was useless as she was escorted out from the chambers by two Sentinels.

CHAPTER EIGHTEEN
SECTION FIVE: ROOK

"Alright!" hollered the Superintendent, "Enough! On yer feet!" Clean-Up Crew Beta One rose from their prone positions to stand at attention. "Now, then!" said the Superintendent, "I don't wanna heah any more bullstuff outta ya'! Is that cleah?! Ah asked if that was cleah?!"

"Yes Sir!!" yelled the crew.

"Dats mo' like it!" admitted the Super, "Now pick up yer tools n' let's get diz toasted bodies onta da' dump truck so's we can git outta heah and back ta' our campus!"

"Yes Sir!!" responded the crew.

"Alright then!" came the order, "Move it out!"

"Beta One Crew One, in effect!" yelled out Squad Leader One.

"Beta One Crew Two, in effect!" yelled out Squad Leader Two.

"Beta One Crew Three, in effect!" yelled out Squad Leader Three.

"Beta One Crew Four, in effect!" yelled out Squad Leader Four.

The teams moved out individually by squads. Ten members were in a squad. Four squads composed a crew. Janno was assigned to Squad Three. Squad Leader Three was called Rex.

"Listen John" Rex said to him, "You keep standards and I'll see what I can do about getting the boss off your back."

"Hey, thanks!" Janno answered, "I would appreciate that."

"No problem" Rex confessed, "Just remember; we all look out for each other out here. If any one of us makes a mistake we all suffer. The day you turn your back on your squad, is the day you find yourself an outcast. Got it?"

"No problem" Janno agreed, "But I'll tell you straight out, I won't do anything contrary to the system."

"Good attitude, Razz" Rex said, "Your with Ruffer, Allen, and Gormely at the shovels. Wear your gloves. We don't want you contracting any diseases from the charred remains of this unit. I'll be back later to check on you guys."

"No problemo', chief-a'-roonee!" Ruffer remarked, "We'll take good care of the Razz. Wont' we guys?"

"Sure thing" Gormely agreed.

"Just do the job right!" Rex ordered. He walked away to lead the rest of his squad to another task. The boys began shoveling dead bodies onto the truck.

"A Rook, huh?" Gormely asked, "He sure knew how to piss Rex off."

"Ease off the Razz" Allen said, "He's from Delta Six. His name's John."

"Delta Six?" Ruffer questioned, "Hey, man, I heard rumors about that place."

"So, I've been told" Janno confessed. He paused for a moment. "I can't help but sense that I have been here before." Ruffer, Allen, and Gormely looked at each other.

"You want to explain what you mean by that?" Gormely asked.

"It's as if I have lived this life before" Janno began to explain, "But somewhere far from here, somewhere different yet the same, a place that is familiar and yet strange. I dream about floating through space and fleeing from an immense dark force that seeks my life."

"Razz?" Ruffer called out to him, "Just do as you're told and everything will be fine, that's all! Dreams are just dreams. Stick to reality and shovel!"

"Can I ask you guys a question?" Janno asked.

"Sure! Go ahead!" Allen agreed.

"What caused all the destruction and the death of these people?" Janno asked.

"Look around you, Razz!" Gormely chastised, "We're being monitored by them!" Janno looked about the ruins of the unit.

Sentinels stood here and there on alert and on guard. They stood in elegant in poise. The sunlight bounced off the smooth coating of their armor. This was the first attention. They scanned about left and right positioning themselves where needed. A Sentinel was graceful in movement. This was the second attention. Though a Sentinel's primary weapon was its enhanced brain filled with options on how to access a situation without the use of violence, they were known to use their laser weapons to keep further violence from occurring. This was the third and final attention. And as the boys worked Rex returned.

"John?" he called out.

"Yes?" Janno answered.

"Your orders came through" Rex announced.

"What?" Janno asked.

"You've been found Fit, Razz" Rex explained, "Take this green arm band and report to the Superintendent. He'll have more instructions for you."

"Fit?" Janno questioned, "Fit for what?"

"You really are a Rook aren't you?" Gormely asked.

"Go on!" Rex ordered, "Get out of here!" Janno left to report to the Superintendent.

"Watch out for the red haired ones!" Ruffer called out to him. Behind Ruffer, Gormely snickered.

"Cut it out you guys!" Allen said, "I'm telling you, he's the one!"

"Huh?" Rex asked, "What do you mean he's the one?"

"That's the Razz from Delta Six!" Allen explained, "The one who we've forfeited sentinel initialization to assist at the Call of Thunder!"

"Oh?" Rex commented, "I'm glad you still think that way."

"What?" Ruffer demanded, "You've got to be kidding, right? I mean, you guys still believe in that old Thunder Storm tale?"

"Wasn't that the reason we all gave up Sentry status and preferred assignment to an institute?" Allen asked.

"Well, actually, I didn't want anyone picking my brain and stealing my identity" Gormely confessed, "But if your right about the Razz and if the theories are

44

true, then we've better stop him from breeding, because if he breeds, he's never gonna reach the metamorphosis. And we'll be stuck cleaning up garbage for the rest of our lives."

"Those are a lot of ifs" Ruffer remarked.

"Listen, guys" Rex said, "That Razz isn't fit for squat didaly-doo."

"What?" Allen asked, "Then why did you grant him the fit band?"

"Yeah!" Gormely demanded, "You should have given it to me!"

"Listen!" Rex clarified, "We need to stop goofing around and get serious. I suspected something to be wrong with that Razz since day one. He's not totally here. Do you understand?

It's obvious that he's missing a piece upstairs."

"Well, heck!" Ruffer said, "Even I noticed that!"

"Oh" Gormely said to him, "In that case something is very wrong with that Delta Six Razz. I mean, even if you noticed!"

"We get the picture, Dumply!" Ruffer expressed.

"That's Gormely!"

"Yo' mama!" Ruffer said.

"Alright you guys!" Rex announced, "Quit the bull!"

"What's a mama?" Allen asked.

"What's a bull?" Gormely Razzed.

"Alright! That's it! Forget it!" Rex said.

"Ok! Ok! We get the message!" Ruffer announced, "But you gotta put yourself in our boots, Rex! We were Sentries once! And we gave all that up because of these tales we were told back in Junior Cycle, Third Stage, Beta Seven! And for what?! To be shoveling dirt and yelled at daily by a derranged son of a b-*!"

"Relax!" Gormely eased as he cut him off, placing a hand over his shoulder, "I'm sure he was reffering to Superintendant Zackery, Rex, but I'm afraid I'll have to agree with him. I mean, how many times have you handed fit bands to anyone you thought to be not really here? You could have saved up those bands, given them to us, and we could've all been long gone by now."

"Why did you give him the band?" Allen asked.

"That's what I been trying to get at!" Rex clarified, "I've checked with Lyman and Taylor, whom we've finally managed to put to work within the communication chambers, at Clean-Up sites, and we've absorbed information we weren't able to have with us before. But if you guys don't take this stuff serious enough, we're going to waste our time and forever live shoveling dung!"

"Alright!" Ruffer exclaimed, "Now you're talking mad lingo'!"

"Taylor plugged into the system's network to verify the rumors we've been hearing concerning Unit Delta Six!" Rex continued, "A band of seniors took the tales to Thunder Storm seriously!"

"What?!" Gormely demanded, "You're kidding!"

"No. I am not" Rex said, "Sentinels converged onto the area and elimnated a few of them. Some were captured and taken prisoners, despite immediate termination orders given by the High Command. They were courted martial and killed off in the end."

"Whoof!" Gormely exhaled, "They really bought the farm, didn't they? For taking the tales seriously?"

"That's not the story" Rex announced, "The point of it all is that the majority of the group busted out to freedom!"

"Freedom!" Ruffer repeated, "It feels like the touch of a forgotten lover upon my skin!"

"But what if we're wrong?" Gormely questioned.

"We mustn't doubt." Allen said.

"The band?" Gormely question, "We need to know about the fit band?!"

"Lyman extracted that information" Rex answered, "Two Delta Six prisoners were taken to Sigma 5. One was Initialized, the other, assimilated and reassigned. And guess where that one landed?"

"Unit Beta Three, Insitute Assigned Janitorial Personnel, Clean-Up Crew Beta One, Squad Three!" Ruffer answered.

"Gee" Gormely expressed, "We're not even good enough to be called a Division!"

"So that's why John's not really with us, right?" Allen asked, "If indeed John really is his name. He's been assimilated." Allen looked towards Ruffer. He paused for moment of thought and then, "Like Ruffer has many times."

"Yeah, now you're getting it," Rex answered.

"Hey?!" Ruffer asked, "What do you mean I've been assimilated?"

"You don't remember. It's why you get nervous when people talk about their dreams," Gormely answered, "You used to come back to us talking a lot about dreams. But the only reason you've managed to recover from your memory loss is because we've kept reminding you about who you are and what you believe in."

"Then you not liking me isn't real? It's just a part of my imagination, right?" Ruffer asked him.

"Oh, no! That part is real," Gormely snickered.

"Jerk!" Ruffer said.

"Come on you guys!" Allen pleaded, "Get serious!"

"Look!" Ruffer explained, "None of you know what it's like to be brain sucked-dry. I almost ended up a vegetable the last time."

"Well, I'm glad you remember" Allen said, "Because

now you can understand what that Razz is going through."

"I still don't get why you sent him via fit band?" Ruffer confessed to Rex.

"One of the court martialed prisoners from Delta Six was returned for breeding procedure and sent to Sigma 5," Rex spoke, "I know it's a long shot, but if those two meet up at Sigma 5, maybe John's memory can return to him. I've only sent him ahead of us."

"You mean we're busting out?!" Ruffer asked.

"You got it! Ruff-a-loonie" Rex said, "I couldn't take the chance of having that Razz come with us in his condition."

"This is too wild!" Gormely admitted, "But I like it. I suddenly don't care if the legends aren't true."

"True or not" Rex spoke, "We were given charges cycles ago. We had better see to it that they are carried out. Ruffer, we'll need some ether for our little trip. Allen, locate layout maps for Sigma 5. Gormely, brush up on your 6-A knowledge. Gentlemen, we have duty to attend to!" Rex stretched his hand out. The others did the same placing their hands above his.

"Beta Seven: Lost Boys?!" they called out, "Execute!" Squad Three, Beta Crew One from Society Unit Beta 3 was composed of an unorthodox Thunder Storm generation. They were outcasts; student personnel who deliberately failed to reach Elite status. They had originated at Society Unit Beta 7. It was here were they came across the beliefs to Thunder Storm. They were considered to be a band of losers. They didn't care for system procedures; not after gaining access to Thunder Storm theories. They had banded together in their third-stage cycle to form an underground society known as "Lost Boys." Dean Joan and Troy had belonged to it, despite their Elite status; for some members of Lost Boys were required to reach Elite rank status, while others were required to fail. Upon Graduation, they were separated and re-assigned to different society units. Yet, before separation, they had vowed to re-unite at the Call of Thunder emerging from Unit Delta Six; or so their plan went.

CHAPTER EIGHTEEN: SECTION SIX
BREEDING ASSIGNMENT

Janno had boarded a transport shuttle. He had been taken to Unit Sigma 5. He thought about his assignment at Unit Beta 3. He was an institute worker. He had free access through the whole of the Beta 3 Third Stage Campus; Vedgil Campus. But he could not remember Delta 6 Graduation, nor transport to Vedgil. The green band he wore around his right arm had granted him entry into Unit Sigma 5. There he had taken another shuttle to the Community Campus of Sigma 5; the Solgi Campus. His arm band had allowed him entry into the Breeding Annex. Inside, he was attended by the Doctors of the System. They had prepared him for the task ahead. Janno had been undressed, cleansed, and tested, to insure that his organs responded properly. He was then oiled and musk so that he emit a strong scent to attract the opposite sex when releasing pheromones.

Janno then waited in a white chamber. It was very peaceful inside. He felt at ease. At the center of the chamber rested a soft padded counter. Janno sat over it and found it to be quite comfortable. He laid down to rest, relaxing his body. He began to fall asleep. Something stirred inside him and suddenly a familiar face caught his attention from the small view of a portal. He rose from the padded counter and hopped up to peer out through the small portal hoping to catch a better glimpse of the familiar face. {I know that face} Janno thought to himself. He watched as a slender girl was escorted by Sentries to his chamber entry. She was being dragged in against her will.

{Watch out for red-haired ones} he thought remembering what Ruffer had yelled out to him. {I wonder what he meant by that?} Janno continued looking out the small elevated window. The slender girl was beautiful. But she was not red haired. She slipped out from the hold of the Sentries and began to run.

One of the Sentries tripped her and she fell to the floor. The Sentries moved in on her but she fought back kicking one of them in the groin. She thrust an open palm into the other's face. Memories stirred inside Janno. He observed the girls maneuvers as she struggled for her freedom. {Analyze?!}, He thought to himself curiously. For a moment it seemed that the beautiful slender girl would win the battle, but then, a Sentinel came. It took hold of the girl and carried her forth. A

Sentry opened the door to Janno's chamber. The Sentinel tossed the girl in. She fell hard to the floor. Janno was displeased. He went to her. "Miss, are you alright?" he asked in an attempt to console her.

"Don't you touch me!" she yelled pushing him away. Janno became upset with the Sentries. For a moment, he suffered to think he had authority over them. He made a move for the door, but it shut immediately before him. Janno sprung to the window. He was about to recall the Sentries and demand that, the doors to the chamber, be opened.

{Just do as you're told and everything will be fine} he remembered Ruffer telling him. He looked at the girl cower in the chamber's corner. He felt scared for her. He wanted to tell her that

59

he was no threat to her but did not know what to say. He had no intentions of going near her. He had seen her take out two Sentries. He did not want to be mistaken for the third.

"I'm really not sure why we were placed in here," he said to her softly, "but I think if we do what we're told, everything will turn out fine. I hope." His voice was very soothing and comforting to her. It was familiar to her. She slowly raised her head and dried her tears with her hands. She looked at him and her heart was filled with joy.

"Janno!!" she yelled. It was Jeena. She sprung from where she sat and wrapped her arms around him. She hugged him fiercely and would not let go.

ℭHAPTER NINETEEN

SECTION ONE: FREEDOM

"𝒢et him out of there!" Peff ordered. Every one moved, Thunder Storm members as well as Warriors. They frantically began to dig for Arco.

"No, wait!" Jeppe called out to them, "It's Ok! It's Ok. I have him encased in the field stasis."

"Razz?" Peff questioned as he dug through the debris, "Are you sure you can get him out of there?!"

"I believe so" Jeppe answered, "I just have to re-connect a few wires in my armor, and cause the electron particles, surrounding the field, to repel off the magnetic polarity encircling the planet, and-"

"Just do it!" Peff told him.

"Ok! Stand back!" Jeppe said, "Here we go!" The mountain of refuse vibrated above the buried Arco. In a few moments a blue bubble appeared. Arco was inside.

Set him down, Razz" Peff requested. Jeppe placed Arco above the debris and released the field stasis. The Warriors went to him and so did some of the medical personnel.

"Oh geez!" Arco remarked, "Geez! I'm shaking."

"Arco?" Yuan asked him, "Are you alright?"

"Oh geez, Razz!" Arco expressed pulling Yuan to him and hugging him, "I thought I was dead! Oh geez, Razz! I'm sorry for the way I've been funning at you?"

"Huh?" Yuan wondered.

"It's Ok, Yuan" Orge said, "The man's shook up."

"You're gonna be alright?" Peff asked him.

"I don't know, boss man" Arco confessed, "I don't know. Too much stuff has happened today and I'm about to crack. Armie is dead. I didn't want to face it, but now I know I have to, just like I have to face every freaking thing that has happened today."

"Hey, man?" Arlos said, "We're alive. We've made it!"

"Don't get your hopes up, pal" Arco warned, "We're not out of the dump hole yet?"

"What do you mean?" Astian asked, "We've kicked butt!"

"Arco makes a point the rest of you fail to understand" Peff explained, "True, it's apparent that we gave the System a good swift kick in the rear, but that's not all we did. We've lost some good people in the process, and darn good people at that. It's the price of freedom to pay for everyone else. If we're going to keep that freedom, we're going to have to destroy the High Command completely; carrying out the duties of Thunder Storm to its fullest, otherwise, the High Command will forever hunt us down. We've just proved that the will of the System is imperfect and in doing so, we've become a force to be patterned after by other people who seek freedom. But if we allow ourselves to be caught and dragged back to the institutes, it shows others that there is no escaping the High Command. We cannot allow that to happen. No. We're gonna show that not only freedom is possible but that the High Command is not omnipotent as we were led to believe."

Peff looked around the junk yard. He looked at the faces of his Warriors and those of Thunder Storm. It seemed everyone had aged rapidly throughout the day. "We're thrashed" Peff confessed, "Alright, listen up everyone. I am Peff, Commanding Officer for the Fighting Force of Thunder Storm. I claim no authority over Luna. She is leader to Thunder Storm and in all cases, I will defer to her. But Luna is injured and needs rest as we all do. And until she can fully recover, I hereby take full charge of the group. We are no longer two separate forces fending for ourselves. We have become one in purpose. Thus we have taken the name Thunder Storm Warriors! We have reached a safe haven. But it will not remain safe for long if we do not take the necessary steps to keep it safe for ourselves. The High Command's control waves will be transmitted to reach our minds and take hold of us once again. We must be ready to fight against that.

I remove these bands from my arm, because these bands tell me that I am a slave. I declare myself a free man and toss these bands to the ground beneath me. If you concede to my temporal authority and are willing to fight for your freedom I ask you then, to remove those Elite bands. Remove those Fit bands and toss them over where I have tossed mine. If you are willing to forsake the will of the High Command and embrace the beliefs of the Most High, then free yourselves and remove those bands!" The squabble team removed their bands and tossed them to the ground. Ace took his off and did the same. Alaetra followed him and soon the others repeated the action. But the junior companions did not know what to do. They were not given bands. They had nothing to throw to the ground to signify their allegiance to Thunder Storm. But, Peff, upon seeing their confusion, spoke again.

"Juniors?!" he called out to them, "It is understood that because of your recent arrival to Third Stage, you could not have received a band. But I tell you that this does not mean that you were not slaves, for I tell you that you were enslaved: enslaved by the infernal regulations of the system. And I tell you that it was with the help of the Most High, whom Chic and Cheynne have spoken to you about, that we were able to find freedom. Wherefore, if you too are willing to enter into the covenant we have made here, this day, raise your right hand high into the sky! Reach out, stretching forth your fingertips as if you were reaching out for freedom, as if you were reaching out to the Most High; He who is your Father. Reach out and cry out with me, Thunder Storm Warriors?!" Peff called out, "Unite!!" And the Junior Companions did lift up their hands and cried out with Peff. And suddenly Peff glowed and metamorphosed before their eyes in the manner the Cheynne had done so at the fourth floor of the Health Annex of the Beaumont Campus in Unit Delta Six.

He shined vigorously and life sustaining force flowed from within him unto the others. They were all rejuvenated. And when it was over, they just looked at one another and marveled.

"I felt that through this Armor" Jeppe confessed noticing the damaged surface to his suit.

"What was that?" Arlos asked with thought, "It's as though I were inside a nutrient capsule, being filled, but with a different kind of nourishment."

"I would proffer and explanation my friends" Orge admitted, "but I'm afraid that this event is beyond my reason of understanding."

"Jeppe?" Astian asked, "Can you tell us what happened?"

"I think" Jeppe answered, "it would be best if we allowed Peff to discuss the matter if he so wishes." Peff had dropped to his knees. He remained unmoving for a while. Nica went to him. She worried for him.

"Do not touch me!" Peff warned her, "I am on fire." And Nica worried for she did not understand. Luna spoke.

"The metamorphosis" she warned, "is a massive release of potential energy in so much that when at peak, it is capable of dissolving through inorganic matter, very much like an acid. The energy is radiated through the pores of the body." Luna became dizzy and held on to her head.

"Is that why Senior Cheynne's clothes burnt off at the medical facility?" Vikki asked.

"His clothes burnt off?" Yuan questioned.

"Why weren't we affected by his radiation?" Ace cut in.

"His radiation was a burst of fire power directed at the Sentinels," Weena answered.

"Well then what do we call Peff's radiation?" Astian sarcastically asked.

Jeppe went to Luna, bracing her shoulders up as she rested on the ground. "Are you alright?" he asked.

"I am now" she whispered softly to him. She continued to explain Peff's condition. "The energy can only interact with living organisms, to mean that it is a life sustaining radiation, not like the ones given off by lethal machines and chemicals. Although touching Peff will not kill you, it will render you neutralized for an extended period of time. Your mind will be overloaded and in a sense, you might short circuit. Cheynne was able to heal the injured. I suspect Peff may be able to do the same, and I also suspect he may be capable of doing a bit more than just that."

"That does appear to be the case" Jeppe confirmed. "Why couldn't I decipher it sooner?"

"Perhaps you're becoming too dependent on that helmet of yours" Luna scolded him playfully "You're to rely on your own knowledge, not computerized readings."

"You're correct, miss" Jeppe agreed, "I'd better remove this armor before I start enjoying its wear." Luna helped him. "I think I should do this alone" Jeppe said.

"Stop being so shy!" Luna said to him. She removed his helmet in time to see him blush. She smiled at him.

"I see you are feeling much better" he said to her.

"It's the healing radiation" Luna confessed, "It's reviving me as well as your presence near me."

"What about Peff?!" Nica asked.

"I think you'd better back away a bit," Orge said to her.

"Why should I?" Nica asked, "Do you think I would hurt him? I love him!"

"That, miss" Orge announced to her, "has been very evident throughout the day. But what I want to point out, is that I have seen enough circuitry overload to know the symptoms, and Peff appears as though he is about to explode any minute."

"Explode?!" Yuan asked worrisome.

"Come closer!" Peff whispered. Everyone was silent. No one moved. "Come closer," he whispered, "All of you gather around me. Form a circle. There are things that you must be made aware of. I will not harm you."

Jeppe picked Luna up in her arms. He walked over to Peff. "I am Ok," Luna whispered to him, "You don't have to carry me. I can walk."

"I know" Jeppe confessed, "But I want to carry you." Luna didn't protest. The others came to sit around Peff who had made a clearing with his radiation.

CHAPTER NINETEEN: SECTION TWO
JOHN OJAHN TWO

And in a reproductive chamber at the breeding annex in Unit Sigma 5: "Miss?!" Janno called out, "Miss?! Please! Control yourself."

"Oh Janno!" Jeena pleaded with him, "Don't play games with me!"

"What?!" Janno demanded.

"It's me! Jeena!" she said.

"I am very pleased to meet you," Janno said releasing himself from Jeena's embrace and extending out a hand. Thoughts of flipping him on to his back, flashed into her mind.

"You had better be playing around!" Jeena said.

"I really am not sure what you're referring to" Janno said.

"Stop it!" Jeena protested, "This is not funny anymore. You're hurting me."

"I don't know what it is I'm doing?" Janno confessed.

"You're pretending not to know who I am," Jeena complained.

"Huh?" he grunted.

"Oh, Janno?!" she asked, "Has it been that long?!" She hugged him and rested her head upon his chest. Janno was confused. He could not let this charade continue.

"Madam!" he spoke, "My name is John! I am an Institute Servant Classified 6-B at the Beta 3 Vedgil Campus! Until a few moments ago, I have never seen your face before in my life."

"What?!" Jeena demanded, "How dare you!" She stepped away from him. She slapped him. Janno's face jerked to the side. His cheek was reddened. He turned to look at her. His eyes squinted, the left one quirked.

"What was that for?!" Janno protested.

"You're going to stand there and pretend we've never met?!" Jeena asked, "You're going to tell me in my face, that after all the wonderful moments we've shared, you have never seen my face, in your life?! Granted, we never slept together! But was that what you needed to always remember me?! Was that all you wanted?! I ought to slap you again!!" Jeena raised her right hand to strike Janno. Janno lifted his left forearm to block Jeena's strike. The speed of his act took him by surprise and he looked at his arm, then back at Jeena. He did not know he could move that fast. She stepped back.

"I will not hurt you," Janno declared to her, "But I would greatly appreciate it, if you would be so kind as to refrain from striking my person until I can better assess my situation."

"Ah...I...I'm sorry," Jeena confessed. She dropped her gaze to the ground. She felt embarrassed. The room suddenly became cold. She turned away from him. Janno returned to the small window.

CHAPTER NINETEEN: SECTION THREE
THE LOST BOYS IN EFFECT

Not too far off in the distance, a transport shuttle was on its way back to its society unit, returning with it, a Janitorial Division: "This is it gentlemen!" Rex spoke, "According to schedule, the transport shuttle's route gets as close to Unit Sigma 5 as this. If we're going to do something, we had better do it now."

"I'm in!" Allen said.

"This is ridiculous, but I ain't got nothing better to do," Ruffer confessed, "Besides it will ruffle the ol' boss man's scalp!"

"Hey!" Gormely exclaimed, "I'm in for that!"

"Get serious you guys!" Rex pointed out, "This isn't a game!" Then he directed himself to two other members of Squad Three. "Lyman! Taylor! Lost Boys, in effect! Are you with us?"

"You're kidding!?" Taylor asked but soon realized that it wasn't a joke, "You're not kidding!! Alright!"

"S'about time!" Lyman answered.

"Good then!" Rex announced, "Gormely, bypass the shuttles directional navigator. We're getting off of this vehicle!"

"Hey what's going on?" another member to Squad Three asked.

"Ruffer!" Rex ordered, "Gas tube in effect! Lost Boys! Filter up!"

"I thought I'd never get to use this!" Ruffer called out. He pulled out a vial from within his jump suit's top arm pocket. The rest of the members to Lost Boys, within squad three, strapped on oxygen masks, removed from their jump suits, over their faces. "Nighty night, Razzdies!" Ruffer exclaimed as he broke the vial within the transport shuttle.

"Gas! Gas! Gas!" yelled a voice. Everyone scrambled and in the excitement Gormely reached the shuttle's navigation unit.

"Let's see now" Gormely spoke to himself, "Screen shield; bypassed. Ahh! There it is. Radar control unit; jammed. Heh-heh! Hmmm? Sure are a lot of wires here. Now how did that old tune go? Oh yeah! The red wire is connected to the blue wire. The blue wire is connected to the yellow wire. The yellow wire is connected to the black wire...Hey?...what about this white wire thing-a-ma-jig...oh? I know! You do the hokey pokey and you turn yourself around..." Gormely was having fun.

"Today, please!" Lyman hollered, "Today!"

"Yeah! These filter masks are not going to last long!" Taylor added. Everyone within the shuttle not member to the Boys began to pass out.

"Well, I can't do everything!" Gormely protested.

"Bust the lock, G!" Ruffered yelled, "Bust the lock!"

"Radar Navigation Control Unit: Temporarily neutralized!" Gormely announced.

"The door!" Rex pointed, "Get the door!"

"Was I the only one who studied electronics?" Gormely asked sarcastically.

"The door, G!" Ruffer said gagging in his mask, "The door!" Gormely bypassed the magnetic shut doors to the shuttle; they opened.

"Lost Boys!" Rex called out, "Dismount!"

"Bonzai!" Allen yelled as he jumped out from within the non-navigational moving transport shuttle.

"Make way!" Taylor called out as he dove through the doors.

"Let's move out, gentlemen!" Rex announced as he followed Taylor.

"I'm not jumping out there!" Gormely protested.

"You don't have to!" Lyman said, taking hold of him, "I'll toss you out!"

"AAAHHH!" Gormely yelled. Lyman followed behind.

"Well if you can't beat them?" Ruffer said, "Bonzai!" All six Lost Boys had jumped out of the returning transport shuttle as it neared Society Unit Sigma 5. The rugged dessert terrain was a new environment for them.

"Hey!" Gormely protested, coughing sand out of his mouth, "This isn't what I pictured the Outer System to be like? Somebody lied to me!"

"Wa-hoo! Ha! Ha! Ha!" Ruffer laughed, "The ol' man's gonna freak when he finds out that we're gone! Ha! Ha!" He paused from laughing to imitate the Superintendant, "Why dem' dirty nah good fer notin' bunch o swine! Haaaaaahhh! Haaaahh! Ha! Ha! Ha! Ha! Ha!"

"Rex?" Taylor said, "That guy's going to lose his mind in the confines of satirical confusion!"

"Get with it, gentlemen" Rex gave the command, "Keep it together. We've got a couple of miles to go before we reach the Unit's perimeters. Allen? Do you have the complex layouts?"

"All Units are constructed the same," Allen answered, "The map I confiscated from the scorched units we were cleaning up earlier will do."

"Good!" Rex announced, "Boys?! Forward: Double time; March!" And they sped on their way.

CHAPTER NINETEEN
SECTION FOUR: REVIVAL

At Sector Chi 7, Quadrant 4; the System's recycling center to which students called the Junk Yard: Life flowed forth freely from Peff and those who sat around him received it. Wounds were healed, strength was replenished, exhaustion was rested, and fear was overcome.

"I speak to all of you as a whole" Peff said to them, "I speak to all of you as individuals. I begin to understand the purpose of our existence. We each have specific tasks to perform in this life. It is a task that must be accomplished or you will not find rest. You cannot run from it but rather face it. I have come to realize that my purpose, our purpose, for now, is to destroy the High Command. For that is why we exist. That is what we were chosen by previous Thunder Storm generations to carry out. My mind has opened and I reveal this unto you that you may be strengthened against the influences of the High Command.

There are some who may ask why I am obsessed with the destruction of the High Command. I tell you that I am not obsessed with destruction, but rather obsessed with self preservation,

preservation for freedom. It is this freedom that you must come to understand. Freedom is a natural unalienable right necessary for progress. But when you are not given opportunity to fulfill self progress, you are oppressed. When this happens, it is vital that the source of the oppression is sought out and dealt with accordingly. If we allow oppression over others to continue, then we are no better than the source of the oppression itself, for we then assist it by covering it up. Negligence does not correct the matter.

I tell you, that the High Command must die, for we have come to understand the type of life we do not want. And that life is one of enslavement at the hands of a machine; at the hands of the System. Many of our tutors, who have undergone Initialization

Sequence, have returned to us as strangers, not knowing who or where they came from. They simply follow orders and we are led to believe at the institutes that this is a life worth striving for. I tell you it is not.

What kind of world are we in that we are forbidden to love? What kind of world are we in that we are forbidden to feel? Are we not humans? Are not emotions parts of being human? What human law upholds that we must become that which is not human? I tell you that if such a law exists, it is not human. And if the law is not human then it is inhuman. And if the law is inhuman then it is not required for humans to adhere to it. For it is not human. And if the law be from the Most High, it cannot be called inhuman, for it is more than human. It is then a Most High Law. And if this be a law for a God, then how much more do we, who are humans, and who are less than a God, have to follow it?

I tell you, we must preserve our freedom. And the only manner in which we shall do that, is if each one of us carries out and fulfills his duty to Thunder Storm, and in doing so, fulfilling our purpose in life. And now, my fellow warriors, I must rest. For even though I have metamorphosed, my metamorphosis is not complete and this body is but flesh and bones subject to the weaknesses and frailties of mortal life...human life. But I ask you to contemplate that which I have spoken to you, for as we have entered into a covenant of preserving freedom, so shall we take the necessary steps to achieve the means.

Therefore, rest now, for the war has just begun and there are many battles yet to fight, and you shall need your strength." One by one, they parted from Peff, to dwell upon the speech addressed to them as a whole and as individuals. Only Nica remained to watch over him as his body began to cool, and the radiation, wear off.

CHAPTER NINETEEN: SECTION FIVE MEMORIES

And at the reproduction chamber at Sigma 5 Solgi Campus Breeding Annex: "As I was trying to tell you earlier" Janno spoke to Jeena as he starred out of the window, "As long as we do what is required of us then everything will be fine."

"What?!" Jeena questioned, "You expect me to-?"

"I do not expect you to do anything," Janno said, "only help me escape from here."

"Huh?" Jeena mumbled.

"Allow me to explain," Janno said, "I have these dreams. They tell me that I do not belong here. They tell me that my life is not what it seems to be. I belong someplace else, but I do not know where."

Jeena turned towards him. She came closer as he continued speaking to her. "Somewhere," he said, "out there lays an important task for me, and yet I cannot know what it is." Janno turned to Jeena. She was standing before him. She was beautiful to him. Familiar but mysterious feelings stirred in him for her. "Am I psychologically impaired?" he asked her.

Jeena looked into his eyes and could see that there was something wrong in him, for he truly could not recognize her. "Who do you think you are?" she asked him.

"I think to be John Ojahn Two from Beta Three Vidgil Campus Institute Assigned Personnel," he answered her.

"That's the problem," she clarified, "You are not!"

"I'm not?" he questioned.

"No. You are not," Jeena confirmed, "Can you remember where you were before Beta Three?"

"I came from Delta Six" Janno answered and for a brief second there was a glimmer of hope in Jeena's eyes.

"I too come from Delta Six," Jeena confessed.

"Then you must know who I really am," Janno said.

"I do," Jeena agreed. Janno looked deep into her eyes. She really was beautiful. He could sense the presence of emotion exist between them.

"Were we...intimates?" he asked her. Jeena then knew. Janno was not playing. He had been assimilated. She did not answer him. She could not look at him. She realized that all the years he had been away, all she ever thought about and hoped for was to be bred with him. It was all she wanted. It was all she desired. She was embarrassed to answer him. She was embarrassed at her accusation of his wanting to use her. She felt ashamed.

{To love, someone, you set them free and all you have is for them to be} Cheynne had explained this to her in her First Cycle of Third Stage. Memories flashed into her mind and she remembered his words. {Love is giving of one self, in a way that is beneficial to another person's progress and purpose in life. Love is not sexual interaction, nor is sex the ultimate means of its expression. Love is of a spiritual nature. It is to guide another towards personal progress; be it mental, physical, in a health related sense, or spiritual. The ultimate expression of loving someone is dying for them. Love is suffered when one is willing to sacrifice one's very life for another, without hope for reward or sexual expectations. This is love.

It hurts when one is abused or taken advantage of. But what

matters is that one can love without permitting oneself to surrender sexually. That is love. When emotion is exhausted and all that there is to give has been given; when there is no energy left, one must seek out a spiritual source that one may be strengthened that one may continue to love. This is ability to love.

And only until all sources have been depleted, can one stop to love. Then one must let go. Until one lets go can one understand love. Letting go is the lesser meaning of expressing love. Actual dying for them expresses the greater meaning.

Once love is had and once it is gone, through experience, it is known how to distinguish between happiness and misery, from joy or pain. Love only goes away to be recognized, appreciated, and not taken for granted. One cannot know what one truly has until after it is gone. How can one know what one has in life if one has not yet lived without?

Guilt and shame come when the love is gone, and it is the consequence of taking love for granted. Torment and the desire to love back are followed. Love is suffered. Subconscious want to be loved in the way one was before is expected. This expectation will not be fulfilled. What will attract, to a new love, will be a memory of the old.

No emotion can come to existence unless it is first accepted, whether the emotion is good or bad. As long as it is rejected it cannot exist. In order for emotion to be accepted, it must be shown for what it truly is, whether good or bad.   This   is   Universal   Law. Universal Laws are Laws of the Spirit.   Spiritual Laws cannot be broken. Spiritual Laws are the Laws of God. Therefore, if one is going to love, love true or do not bother to love at all.} Janno took hold of Jeena's arms.

"You are hiding something" he said, "Please tell me. I need to know who I am." Jeena braced his arms.

"You must be strong" she said. She   took   him   to   the   padded counter and made him lie down.

"What are you going to do?" he asked her.

"Nothing" she answered, "It is you who will be doing all the work. Just listen to my voice. I will guide you. Now close your eyes." Janno closed his eyes.

"I shall talk you through a process of relaxation techniques that you may meditate and find the answers to your identity locked away inside your mind. Which is why, you must be strong, because we do not know what we will find in there. There may be hidden commands locked away in your subconscious, commands that, we do not know what may result, should we come across one. It is possible that there exists a self-destruction program sequenced in your brain, a program that may be activated by one simple word."

"Such as?" Janno asked, opening his eyes.

"We don't want to find out!" Jeena scolded him.

"I'm not sure I want to go through with this" Janno admitted.

"You were always unnerved by psychological games," Jeena reminded him.

"Unnerved?" Janno questioned, "It seems you do know much about me. Are you calling me a coward?"

"I said no such thing," Jeena answered.

"Do you know me to be a coward?" he asked her.

"No," she responded. He looked at her and she was pleasing.

"I'm concerned for your safety" Janno said, "I don't know what I may do to you, for I find you extremely pleasing to look at." Jeena blushed. "I am not sure if I were the type to force himself on someone."

"Trust me!" Jeena said, "You were not!" Janno took one last look at her then he closed his eyes. He laid flat on the padded counter. It was very comfortable. Jeena stood behind the head of the counter. She gently placed her hands over his temples and began to massage them. She spoke softly to him. "The brain" she said, "is the primary part of the nervous system. Will you repeat that, please?"

"The brain is the primary part of the nervous system," Janno repeated.

"A neuron is the most important cell in living organisms," she continued, "Please repeat that as well."

"A neuron.. is.. the.. most.. important cell... in.. living... organisms ...", Janno repeated sleepily as Jeena continued to work on his temples.

"The neuron is the cell responsible for memory," Jeena continued, "Neurons compose memory input stored within the brain." Janno slowly repeated her words until he fell asleep. Jeena continued talking to him, "Neurons contain knowledge genetically inherited from our ancestors. We shall explore each memory stored within your mind until we find one that truly belongs to you, and then we can enhance its knowledge, and hopefully awaken your true self...."

CHAPTER NINETEEN: SECTION SIX
LUNA TAKES CHARGE

And back at Sector Chi 7, Quadrant 4, the System's Recycling Center, the Thunder Storm Warriors began to prepare for their attack on the High Command.

"Warriors?!" Peff called out, "Unite!" At his call, Thunder Storm came to rally themselves around him. Peff had recovered. His metamorphosis was at an early stage and would come and go every now and then until it reached completion.

His clothes did not burn off for it had his own sweat as did the others had their respective sweat that the energy would not destroy for it was an organic energy. Cheynne's was a different case. His was solar.

"We have had enough time to rest and recuperate from our

previous battle with the System," he said, "I want to start on preparing our battle strategy that we may have a chance at victory. I ask Luna to concur with this meeting."

"I concur" Luna agreed, "We have all taken an oath to follow your lead until I regained full recovery. I have done so, yet because of the nature of what we're about to do, I would prefer that your experience in battle remain our guide and thus step down as leader to Thunder Storm and defer command of the group towards you."

"I second the motion," Orge said.

"I decline," Peff announced, "I understand why you wish I should take charge, but I want to point out that war and destruction should not be our only purpose.

We must begin to build a future for ourselves. When the High Command is defeated, we must maintain order and establish a way of life. We need laws and regulations to insure that nothing like enslavement of the System comes into effect ever again."

"I have a projective USB drive that contains data from some discs that belong to Janno," Jeppe spoke, "They have in them several ancient texts concerning government. I believe they may help us. We need Janno."

"Most of us are inexperienced in combat," Peff said, "Those who are not should remain behind here at Sector Chi 7, Quadrant 4, to start building a future. There's plenty of raw material at hand. I'm sure with Jeppe's assistance, anything can be built.

The frequency shield must come into effect to keep the frequencies of the High Command away from this area. There is much to do and the weight of responsibility must be shared by all."

"Are you suggesting we have no leader?" Luna asked.

"I think it would be best if we break ourselves down into groups," Peff suggested, "Everyone should be assigned to a group depending on the specific ability of the individual. Each group should have a leader to take charge of a given task. We should elect a representative to speak for the group at Thunder Storm meetings held to check on our progress and to insure that we are indeed ready to take on the System, and I elect that representative be you, Luna."

"I retract my previous endorsement and second this motion," Orge announced jokingly justifying himself.

"Then it's settled. I remain leader to Thunder Storm," Luna agreed. An intangible force coalesced around the group. Everyone felt it. Luna was aware of the amount of responsibility weighing on her shoulders, but she did not waste any time in assigning duties. "Arlos, and Astian?!" she called out. "Since you were once Clips of a Squabble Team, it is logical that the battle strategy task should be given to you that your knowledge, education, and experience in this specific matter may take effect."

In effect!" answered the boys.

Arco and Orge?!" Luna continued, "I need both of you to

remain vigil at the perimeters of the Sector. There should be another refuse truck arriving shortly. Confiscate the truck and scout the position of the System. I need to know what's going on out there."

In effect!" they answered.

Peff?" Luna ordered, "I want you to take charge of this group. Insure that the truck is confiscated then approve the strategic plan for presentation to Thunder Storm. Supervise Yuan."

In effect!" Peff answered. And Luna kept ordering as only a woman could. "Jeppe?" she called out to him, "I need your suit."

What?!" he questioned.

I want duplicates made for all Thunder Storm Warriors. I do not want anyone else dying in battle. Queen and Alaetra will analize it and re-produce it for the others, with your approval of course?"

"Of course," Jeppe repeated in a mocking tone of agreement.

"I then need you to assist me in constructing the frequency shield," she said.

"Yes m'am," Jeppe agreed, with a smile that made Luna blush. She had to turn away from him.

"Ace?" she called out, "I need you to recover raw material for the constructions of these suits."

"You got it!" Ace answered.

"Yuan, Weena, and Chic?" she continued, "Please take charge of our junior companions. Weena will educate them on

Thunder Storm beliefs, and Yuan will train them in self defense techniques to prepare them for what's to come."

"Understood," Chic agreed.

"Yes," Weena said.

"In effect!" Yuan answered.

"Nette, Nica, Betty, and Vette?" Luna commanded, "I need you to run Physical Exams on everyone and locate individual deficiencies that they may be corrected."

"Will do," Nette answered for them.

"That's all for now," Luna finished, "I want to meet again before the night is over. Thunder Storm Warriors: Disperse!" Everyone moved out to carry their specific functions. Night was closing in on them. It was their first time out in the environment. Many were not accustomed to exposure. The medical personnel were aware of that. They were also aware that they had no supplies.

"Man!" Arco commented, "That's some tough chic!"

"What?" Chic asked.

"No, baby, not you," Astian clarified, "He was not referring to you."

"Oh," she said.

"Peff?!" Nica called out to him, "Do you have a few minutes? I need to talk with you."

"Of course" Peff answered, "What can I do for you?"

"Well, first of all" she said, "You can stop being so formal. Second, we need some medical supplies. Perhaps the boys can pick some up during their scouting of the system?"

"I'll have to check with Luna" Peff answered, "Will there be anything else?"

"Peff?!" she whined, "Why won't you talk to me like you used to?"

"I'm changing," he answered her and walked away.

CHAPTER NINETEEN: SECTION SEVEN
THE FATHER

And at a different point in time and space: {Where am I?} Janno thought to himself, {I have been here before and I know this place.}

[I'm right behind you] said a voice. Janno turned to face the voice. A figure garbed in robes of the High Command Council stood before him.

{I recognize you} Janno said.

[I should hope so] said the Counselor, [I am you; Joe Adam Lezama.]

{I had suspected as much} Janno said, {would you care to explain what's going on here?}

[It will be my pleasure] agreed the Counselor, [But I must ask you to hold your questions until I am through or you will prevent a full disclosure of information from occurring.]

{Agreed} Janno said.

[We share common genes. I am your ancestor. Our genetic makeup is identical and so you are easily able to access your memory banks and come in contact with me] said the Counselor, [I am your Father] explained the Counselor, [You are free to ask questions now.]

{Are you God?"}

[God is a title.]

{How did you come to obtain such title? How did you come to be?}

[I did not come to be. I have always existed. I obtained my title upon being actualized in the present and therefore as present time is constant, I have always existed.]

{If you are my Father} asked Janno, {why did you wait so long to tell me?}

[You were too insistent on servicing the System of the High Command. You were not ready to accept such knowledge. I'm being blocked off by the frequencies of the High Command, for if you were permitted to reach me, the High Command and its System will become insignificant to you. That is why you are kept oppressed by a series of contradicting regulations that you may be kept ignorant.]

{Ignorant of what?}, Janno asked.

[Ignorant of who you are,] answered the Counselor. [Ignorant of your purpose, Ignorant of actualization. You are to take my place and I will ascend in glory for you and those who have taken the group name, Thunder Storm are my children.]

{I am not who I think I am, am I?} Janno asked.

[Who do you think you are?], asked the Counselor.

{John Ojahn Two?} Janno answered.

[You are Janno Ojahn One] clarified the Counselor, [You were chosen to block the High Command from spreading its controlling frequencies throughout the universe because of your genetic makeup. You are in my image. My genes were introduced covertly into the master control monitor that became the High Command and you and your fellow Thunder Storm members are the result.

The earth's pollution, the radiation from devices, and the contamination of the waters served to slowly enhance the endurance of mankind. Man slowly evolved to become immune to such hindrance. Abram and I calculated the time and conditions where our genes would manifest to produce posterity through the High Command's bio engineering that would result in super evolved beings that would emanate radiation lethal to the System. You are the Liberator, bioengineered to project your thoughts through time and space.

There is much you must learn but we are nearly out of time, for you see, despite the ability to project your thoughts into space, this is a far as you are able to project. The universe is cordoned off by eight existing pyramids, located at the ends of it, to keep the High Command frequencies from reaching further into this dimension.

These pyramids are energy transmitters and were placed in function by you, as you thought action into existence, while undergoing Assimilation Sequence at Unit Sigma 5. It was there where we last lost contact. In the end no matter who tries to change us we become what we are meant to become. You were shoved onto a different locale in time and space; a deep portion within your mind or space that no one can touch or reach but you and those you are close to.

You love Jeena Ojahn Six. She has been your friend and companion since First Stage. It is she who has enabled you to reach me. Now this is the important part:

I need Thunder Storm's help to return to earth and destroy the High Command.]

{How?} Janno asked

[Thunder Storm must build a tracking system. I will send the proper codes at a designated time to one of the members. In the mean time you must escape. Let me once again escort you through the void.]

{Blessed Oblivion!} Janno said.

HAPTER TWENTY

SECTION ONE
THE PERIMETERS OF SIGMA 5

"*There* it is!" Rex pointed out, "The perimeters to Unit Sigma 5, where we were born!"

"This is going to be fun!" Gormely expressed.

"This is a serious matter!" Taylor said, "Much of our history lies behind those walls."

"How are we going to get in?" Ruffer asked.

"Refuse Transport Shuttles leave the unit every two sessions," Allen answered, "We can enter through when the gates slide open to let the shuttle out."

"Provided of course, we're not seen by Sentinels," Lyman said.

"Naturally!" Gormely agreed.

"We'll have to board the incoming transport," Ruffer suggested.

"Catch it on the way in," Lyman added.

"Agreed!" Rex announced, "Allen, how long before a refuse transport shuttle returns?"

"About point five session," Allen answered, "According to the map layouts from the units we were cleaning up earlier, if we angle at twenty-two point five degrees due east, we should be able to intercept one at its route within a quarter session, taking for account the terrain we're traveling in."

"Good!" Rex said "Boys! We're going to board that shuttle and once we're inside: Taylor, Allen, Ruffer: you three are to locate our birth records. Lyman, Gormely: you're with me. We're going to rescue John and meet up with everyone else at the Master

Assimilation Monitor at one point five session from the moment we infiltrate the unit's perimeters. Synchronize your timers! On my mark, high noon on three! One, two, three!" And with a brief but well thought out plan, the Lost Boys continued their march towards the refuse transport shuttle.

CHAPTER TWENTY: SECTION TWO
THE JUNK YARD

And at the System's Recycling Center, sector Chi 7, quadrant 4: "How's your thigh, Arlos?" Orge asked.

"Deep fried," he answered, "That razz, Vikki, patched me up after Nica and Vette looked me over."

"This first name basis thing is going to take some time to get used to," Astian said.

"It's better than being labeled," Arco expressed.

"Vette seemed to be holding it together. Considering the trauma she suffered at the Beaumont Campus," Arlos commented, "I wasn't sure that I wanted her examining my leg, but Nica assured me it was safe. Of course, I could sense something was troubling her too." He looked towards Peff. Peff understood what he meant but changed the direction of the conversation.

"You put up a good fight back at the Health Annex," he told Arlos, "I think we all did, but the battle isn't over. We need to come up with an attack plan to go up against the System."

"Well, if we were trained correctly as sentries," Orge said, "then memorized geographical layouts learned from Geography Session, should tell us that the nearest unit complex to sector Chi 7, quadrant 4 besides Delta Six is Unit Sigma 5, a medical station." There was a moment of pause.

"That's where we were raised," Arco announced, "where we became Safeties at the Hoover Institute and later shipped out to a Second Stage institute. I could care less if we blow up that place!"

"I share your sentiments exactly, Arco," Peff agreed, "But Sigma 5 houses important information that could be useful to us."

"If only Janno were with us," Arlos said.

"Unfortunately, he is not," Orge said, "Whatever we decide to do must be done without him."

"We've been doing things without him," Arco said.

"I meant we could use some help in obtaining our birth records," Arlos said.

"And the answers to our existence," Astian added.

"We exist to be free!" Orge commented.

"I meant that we would know whom we descend from," Astian clarified, "as well as who is kin to us."

"Exactly!" Peff agreed, "That's why we can't destroy Sigma 5. Its medical purpose is too valuable for us to destroy."

"I am kin to Janno," Astian commented, "We have different mothers."

"Excuse me," Arco cut in, "but even if we wanted to it seems very much impossible that six outlaw sentries, a whiz razz, and a rag-tag band of fugitive students could destroy such a place."

"Arco, I know you're upset about a lot of things," Peff said, "But we have to keep together."

"How about we just capture the place then?" Arco suggested.

"That's not such a bad idea!" Orge announced, "It would be a piece of cake to do so with that frequency shield the Luna girl and that Jeppe razz are building."

"Of course!" Astian exclaimed, "By blocking out the High Command frequencies, the whole place would shut down."

"Chaos would run amok!" Arlos said, "We would have to situate thousands of students breaking loose from three campuses."

"It sounds like a Sentinel matter to me," Peff remarked, "Maybe we can sneak into the unit and shut down the Sentinel Division only. They would be our only threat within the outer system."

"What about the campus' militia?" Arco warned, "Safeties, Scouts, and Sentries? We can't take them all on even if we deactivate a Division of Sentinels."

"Perhaps we can infiltrate," Orge announced.

"What do you mean?" Peff asked.

"If some of us can get into the campuses," Orge explained, "we can have them impart Thunder Storm beliefs onto the other students."

"Then the rest of us can hit the unit's central core chambers where the Digit One is kept," Astian concluded, "And upon shutting down the system at Unit Sigma 5 all other non-initialized personnel would understand what's going on."

"It's all too easy!" Arco confessed, "When I said I would fight to the dirty end, I meant I didn't care about how fair it was going to be. But considering what we're up against, I'm not opposed to using any means available to us. Only I question the dump truck confiscation. Wouldn't that alert the High Command to our location?"

"What if we use a frequency shield," Arlos pointed out, "to capture the truck and then somehow send messages to the High Command to make it seem that everything is running in perfect order?"

"That sounds like a good idea!" Astian said.

"I like it too!" Peff agreed, "Which means that we'll need Jeppe or Luna to build us a quick frequency shield. Orge? Arco? You two will be the first to have squabble suits made. They resemble sentinel armor, and since it requires both of you to scout the system before us, I see no reason why we shouldn't minimize the risks and have you both sent in as Sentinels."

"Sentinel status!" Astian said, "Far out!"

"Arlos? Astian?" Peff continued, "You two review the battle plans and make sure that there are no glitches. We can't afford to suffer any mistakes."

"In effect!" they answered.

"I'll check with Luna and Jeppe to request a portable frequency shield," said Peff, "not to mention the request to have squabble suits made for us first."

"What do we do in the meantime?" Arco asked.

"Hey?!" Orge said, "We can help locate suitable material for Ace, Queen, and Alaetra. They can look us over for measurements and proper fitting!"

"Agreed!" Peff said.

"In effect!" they responded. And the once Sentries, now Thunder Storm Warriors broke off into their perspective groups to carry out their duties.

CHAPTER TWENTY: SECTION THREE
LUNA AND JEPPE

And within the same quadrant: "Luna?" Jeppe called to her, "Cut it out!"

"You do not like it when I touch you?" she asked him.

"I don't mind you touching me" Jeppe said, "but pinching into my waist line beneath my ribs is somewhat distracting."

"You're ticklish!" Luna announced and she reached out to tickle him.

"Don't you dare!" Jeppe warned, "I'm right in the middle of an inter-crossing wire connection. We could get electrocuted." Luna pulled back.

"Oh?" she said and after a moment of thought she asked, "Don't you like me?"

"Of course I do," he answered her, "I find you most appealing."

"Then why won't you touch me?" she asked, "You make me feel repulsive when you won't touch me."

"You shouldn't think that way" Jeppe told her, "I've carried you, had your hip taken care of, and done what else I could to look after you. What else would you have me do for you?"

"Would you kiss me?" Luna asked shocked at the conversation she was having with Jeppe. Jeppe stopped from the work he was doing to look at Luna.

"You are very beautiful to me," he said, "I would very much like to kiss you but I do not know how to kiss a...a damsel, and liberty cannot afford the time right now for me to stop doing what I'm doing to learn how to. We have much work to do and I cannot risk it."

"Jeppe?" Luna questioned, "What will you be putting at risk if you kiss me?"

"I don't know," he confessed, "but I think we should continue working on this field platform." Just then Peff came to them.

"Peff?!" Luna cried half startled, "I didn't see you coming."

"I'm sorry to have taken you by surprise," he said, "I came by to relate our battle plans to you and to request your assistance."

"What can we do for you?" Luna asked.

"Our battle plans require a portable frequency shield to intercept the next incoming transport shuttle," he answered.

"Oh?" Luna said. She looked to Jeppe.

"We also need a special transmitter to transmit the High Command frequency code to cover our attacks, not to mention a couple a communicators" Peff quickly added.

"I see no problem" Jeppe said, "Communicators are being built into the squabble suits and special adaptors can be made to imitate Sentinel transmission. But I understand that you'll need one for the transport shuttle. I can have that ready for you within a half a session."

"Thanks, Jeppe!" Peff said, "The next shuttle arrives within point seven five session." Peff looked to Luna. "I wanted to request that squabble suits for Arco and Orge be constructed ASAP as they will be scouting the system ahead of us. I don't want to send them in exposed to harm. They can infiltrate as Sentinels."

"That's a wonderful idea!" Luna said, "I'll inform Alaetra and Queen." She paused to look at Jeppe. "Uh, Jeppe?" she called to him.

"Yes?" he answered.

"I'll be right back to continue our...ah...conversation?" she said.

"...as you command..." Jeppe answered her.

"Thank you, Luna" Peff said and he walked away to keep an appointment with the medical personnel who wanted to examen him.

CHAPTER TWENTY: SECTION FOUR
JANNO'S RETURN

Sanity was his once again, but he knew that part of him was still missing and held captive at the assimilation monitor. Janno found himself within the breeding annex of the Solgi Campus at Unit Sigma 5. Jeena was above and behind him, slowly massaging his temples as he rested on a padded counter within the center of the room. They were supposed to be breeding by orders of the High Command. They were not.

"Jeena?" he called out to her.

"Janno?" she questioned.

"Yes!" he answered, "It's me. I'm back!" He sat up on the counter. She came over to him. He dropped to the floor from the counter and hugged her. "Jeena!" he said.

"Oh, Janno!" she cried, "I've been so scared. I thought I would never ever see you again. I've been so scared."

"It's alright!" he reassured her, "Everything is going to be fine. I promise. I won't let anything happen to you." She hugged him tightly. She didn't want to let go.

Tears formed around her eyes. He wiped them away. "Jeena, how long have we been in here?"

"Nearly two sessions," she answered.

"Jeena?" he said, "We have to get out of here."

"I know," she said, "But I don't know how?"

Janno realized she was crying. He cupped her face in his hands and brushed away her hair to expose her eyes. He wiped away her tears and kissed her gently on each cheek. "I need you to be strong, now," he said to her, "I saw you take out two sentries earlier. That was pretty brave of you."

"Thank you," she said, "I couldn't have done it if you never would have taught me how."

"I'm glad I did," he said.

"Me too," she agreed. She smiled and her beauty caused him to smile as well. They hugged each other.

"Jeena?" he said to her, "In a few moments, the Sentries guarding us outside the doors will be coming in to check up on us and verify if we have completed our assignment. The High Command will stimulate our bodies through frequencies directed into the cerebral cortex within our brains. I don't know how to counteract it. We'll soon have an immense sexual desire for each other. We have to be careful. I can sense my testosterone levels increasing."

"Janno, I thought I always held sexual desires for you," she abruptly said then covered her mouth not believing that she had said what she did.

"No. Jeena" Janno corrected her, "It isn't your genuine thought. It's what the High Command wants you to believe. Now stand over here," he told her placing her at the side of the door way. "I'll be at the other side of the door way. When the Sentries walk in, we'll attack them." She looked at him. She loved him. She told him so. "I love you Janno!" she said to him. They were not the words he expected to hear at the moment but they fortified him.

"I know," he answered her, "I feel the same way." And with affections exchanged they both braced themselves up against the wall opposite each other at the side of the door way.

CHAPTER TWENTY: SECTION FIVE
INTO THE DESERT

The sound of the engine traversing across the terrain was deafening. At close range, the sound became louder. They signaled each other while placing mini ear transmission plugs. "Here it comes!" Allen called out, "Right on schedule!"

"Alright everybody: ready yourselves!" Rex called out, "On my mark! Forward thrust! Move!" The Lost Boys jumped out from beneath the sand dunes and rushed towards the oncoming Refuse Transport Shuttle (RTS). Normally a shuttle would be traveling a lot faster than anyone would be able to board it, but due to the desert terrain the vehicle moved slower and so it was feasible for the Boys to hop upon it. One by one they boarded the shuttle.

"It's like hopping a train!" Ruffer yelled.

"You've never hopped a train!" Gormely yelled back.

"I saw pictures!" Ruffer defended himself.

"Well, you look like a hobo!" Gormely chided.

"What's a hobo?" Ruffer asked.

"Bad news!" Allen called out.

"Bad news?!" Gormely questioned.

"No," Allen clarified, "Bad news!   We're on the wrong transport shuttle!" He jumped off.

"What?!" Rex demanded.

"This truck is heading away from Sigma 5!" Allen yelled from the ground.

"We had better jump off and onto the returning transport!" Lyman hollered, "Here it comes! If we miss this one, we're not going to be of any use to John and neither will he be, to us, if he breeds!" Lyman threw himself off of the shuttle and prepared himself to board the correct RTS.

"We can cross jump from where we are!" Taylor yelled, as he dove from one truck and onto the other. He landed on the forepart of the oncoming shuttle. Rex, after jumping, barely managed to hoist himself onto the end part of the correct transport. And from the ground Allen and Lyman boarded the sides of the RTS without any risk.

Only Gormely and Ruffer were unable to jump. The double-time-march, run earlier had exhausted their energies. They couldn't co-ordinate for the moment and had they been able to, timing would not have allowed them to make the jump. They stayed on top the outgoing shuttle.

"Dangit!" Rex exclaimed.

"What do we do now?" Allen asked.

"We keep going!" Rex answered.

"Those two are going to kill each other," Taylor said.

CHAPTER TWENTY: SECTION SIX
SELF DEFENSE

And at sector Chi 7, quadrant 4: "That's it!" Yuan encouraged, "A forward thrust kick to the abdomen can bring an opponent into a position where you can execute a second kick into his face."

"With which leg?" Angie asked, "The right or the left?"

"Well that's going to depend on which leg you use initially to kick your opponent's abdomen," Yuan answered.

"Could you demonstrate for us?" Deena asked.

"Sure!" Yuan agreed. "If you kick in with your right leg," he said, "follow through stepping into your kick, then rotate your body to the left. Swing your left leg to the rear, pivot left with your right foot then bring your left foot to your buttocks to balance yourself as you continue your rotation. Take aim as to where you want to kick and strike with the left!"

"Good move!" applauded Peff.

"Peff?!" Yuan said, "Thank you."

"If I startled you, my apologies" Peff said, "I seem to be moving in upon people without being noticed since my metamorphosis began."

"That might be useful to us in a fight," Yuan said. "What can we do for you?"

"Nette wants to run a medical on you again," Peff answered.

"Again?" Yuan questioned, "This will be the third time today."

"I guess she just wants to make sure," Peff said.

"Yes, but make sure of what?" Yuan asked.

"That she likes you!" Tina blurted out.

"Tina!" Luani called, "That's between seniors!"

"It's Ok," Yuan said, "No offense is taken, Luani. I'll be going to my medical checkup and Peff here will continue where we left off."

"Uh, how far are you?" Peff asked.

"Well, ah? We've gone through punches, blocks, kicks, and offensive attacks" Yuan said.

"Good!" Peff said, "We'll continue with defense and counter attacks. Oh and Yuan, there's a truck coming in within less than point thirty-five session. We'll need to rendezvous for confiscation."

"Understood!" Yuan said then re-phrased himself, "Ah, I meant...in effect!"

CHAPTER TWENTY: SECTION SEVEN SENTINEL STATUS

Meanwhile, not too far away: "This will be your chest plate," Queen said to Orge, "You've grown a bit since we last met."

"I try to keep in shape," Orge announced, "I would like to say the same for you but I'm afraid I might be misinterpreted."

"Thank-you for being considerate," Queen said to him.

"What are these things made out of?" Arco asked.

"They're forged out of a special kind of alloy that will help shield you from low density lasers," Alaetra answered him.

"What do you mean low density?" Arco asked.

"Sentry stun weapons," Ace clarified.

"Jeppe was able to analyze one of the weapons earlier and reduce it to its components, we reversed engineered one." Queen said, "We were then able to make duplicates and install them into your battle suits and alter them to high density to resemble Sentinel laser."

"This is an awesome feeling," Arco admitted, "To be made into a Sentinel but without losing your identity. This is how it should have been in the first place."

"There!" Ace announced, "That should just about do it."

"You guys look great!" Alaetra said, "Stand up. Let's see if you can move about." Orge and Arco stood up to move around.

"This is going to take some time to get used to," Orge said, "No wonder Sentinel's move slowly."

"I love these boots!" Arco confessed.

"I'm still somewhat confused about the laser shielding part" Orge said.

"Put your helmets on and we'll explain that to you," Ace told him. "The way the suits are constructed, they will repel off any minimum heat energy, even such concentrated into a laser. At low density, energy within the Sentry Stun Weapons is concentrated into cool color neutralizing light. These will bounce off the mirrored alloy. A Sentinel's laser blast is a bit denser in that the concentration of energy is greater than a stun weapon's as the density is compacted into cool colored light. Cool colored lights carry more photons than a warm colored light. So we built in something extra to keep out the photons. If you press the blue button at your left palm, an electric magnetic shield will form around you."

"Hey?!" Arco exclaimed, "This is like that blue stasis thing that Razz kept saving everybody with."

"Hold still!" Queen said, "We're going to hit you with these pipes."

"What?!" Orge protested.

"The blue button!" Alaetra yelled, "Hit the blue button!" And she smashed a pipe against Orge's helmet. It bounced off and out of her hands.

"Hey, that's neat!" Arco exclaimed, "What does the white button do?" He pressed it and beneath his feet he could sense something lift him into the air. "Whoa!" he yelled as he was flipped over onto his back, "What was that supposed to be?"

Anti-gravitational boots that repel you off the electric field encircling the planet" Ace explained, "Sentinels do not have this, so you'll have to use it in emergency situations only, or you'll blow your cover."

That's like the blue bubble thing that saved me from the falling debris when we first got here, right?" Arco asked.

You got it!" Alaetra answered.

Ok, now, I have two buttons on my left palm" Orge said, "The blue one I can reach with my index and middle fingers, and it's for electromagnetic shielding against high density lasers. The white one, I can reach with my ring finger and pinkie and it's for levitation. Right?"

"That's right!" Queen answered.

"What are the red and yellow buttons on my right palm for?" Orge asked.

"The yellow one is for radar jamming against the high command's frequency" Ace answered, "At the same time it emits similar High Command frequencies to blend in with the System's signals. Luna brought us the designs earlier just before we began installing the electrical circuits within the suits. The red button is for laser use. Communicators are built into the helmets."

"Hey, Arco?!" Orge called out, "You want to wrestle?"

"Oh no!" Alaetra said, "I knew this was going to happen!"

"Ease up, babe!" Ace said, "It'll give them a chance to test out the suits. Knock yourselves out, you guys!"

"I don't like this rough housing" Queen said, "I'm going to take a break."

CHAPTER TWENTY: SECTION EIGHT ALLIANCE

And up atop a Refuse Transport Shuttle: "Well, you got any bright ideas?" Gormely asked.

"It will be point five sessions before we start heading in the right direction" Ruffer explained, "It will take us another session to get through the perimeters of Unit Sigma 5. By that time, the rest of the Lost Boys should be gathered at the Master Assimilation Monitor and moving on out."

"We don't even know where the Master Assimilation Monitor is housed," Gormely pointed out.

"Didn't you hear what Allen was saying about all unit layouts being the same?" Ruffer questioned.

"So?" Gormely commented.

"So, where was the Master Assimilation Monitor kept back at Unit Beta 7?" Ruffer asked. "How should I know?" Gormely questioned, "You were the one who was taken there often."

"You were taken there once!" Ruffer announced.

"Was not!" Gormely protested.

"Was too!" Ruffer insisted.

"All right!" Gormely confessed, "I was taken there but just once! I don't recall its location."

"It is located two miles west of the Unit's Central Core Chambers!" Ruffer answered.

"So where are the Central Core Chambers kept?" Gormely asked.

"Where else?" Ruffer answered, "Right smack at the center of the Unit, surrounded by Sentinel Division Head Quarters. That's where we'll be going or at least in that direction to get back with the rest of the group. Listen, do you think you can run interference on this vehicle and get us moving back to Sigma 5?"

"Hey?!" Gormely exclaimed, "It'll be worth a try. You'll have to help me remove the forward panels though."

"Deal!" Ruffer agreed.

CHAPTER TWENTY: SECTION NINE ESCAPE

And at the Breeding Annex of Unit Sigma 5: The doors slid open. Janno took the Sentry by the shoulders and planted his right knee into his abdomen. He fell forward rolling onto his back bringing the Sentry with him and then Janno tossed the other one over and on to his respective back. The Sentry fell with a loud thud. He was out cold. Jeena simultaneously thrust her elbow into the second Sentry's gut. She struck her palm downward onto the Sentry's groin. She struck once more bringing her elbow up to the Sentry's jaw. He fell back as she punched him in the face with the back of her fist. Jeena quickly dragged him inside by his feet. "That was close!" she said.

"It's a good thing they were Clips; small and light weight" Janno said, "I don't think that we could have done so well had the Sentries been Mediums or Strongs."

"I think we were in luck!" Jeena concluded.

"Close your eyes, Jeena" Janno said, "I'm going to exchange uniforms with this Sentry and then hopefully lead us out of here." Jeena closed her eyes as Janno exchanged uniforms. She thought about all of the events that had brought her to where she now was. She remembered being called for breeding at Reunion Session. She remembered the generation's first Thunder Storm meeting. She remembered how they had to disband because of Sentinel investigation; how the Sentries did battle against a Sentinel.

It all seemed so long ago and yet she could recall every detail. She recalled Thunder Storm's second meeting at the medical facility. It was there were she had borrowed Luna's sensor to track Janno down. She recalled almost being raped by a Strong Sentry, Dogger: how she had struggled greatly for her virtue. She recalled being rescued by Assistant Dean Troy and Dean Joan. Troy had been killed and both she and Dean Joan had been captured by the invading Sentinels at the Beaumont Campus Unit Delta 6. She remembered Stick Shift. How he related to her the battle of the fourth floor of the Health Annex, how Cheynne had metamorphosed into a being better suited for the conditions of life. The beliefs to Thunder Storm were true. They were being enslaved by the will of a superiorly evolved computer program gone haywire. They were limited to what they can do. This she witnessed at the High Command's Central Core Chambers where Cheynne and Stick Shift were both put to death. She thought about Cheynne for a while. She loved him so. He was her dearest friend. But, Dean Joan! Dean Joan had been sentenced to assimilation! This thought shocked her into the present. "Janno!" she called, "Janno!"

"What is it?" Janno asked zipping up his light blue jump suit, "What is it?"

"Dean Joan!" Jeena cried, "She's going to be assimilated! We

have to help her! We have to
rescue her!"

CHAPTER TWENTY: SECTION TEN
RESCUE PLAN

And somewhere nearby:
"We're past the perimeters!" Rex
called out, "Remember! We're
keeping up with the same plans.
Nothing has changed. We will
meet up at the Master Assimilation
Monitor one point five session from
now. Monitor your timers! Prepare
to dismount! Dismount!" The Lost
Boys hopped off the incoming
transport shuttle at Unit Sigma 5.
Rex and Lyman made way
towards the breeding annexes of
the Solgi Campus to rescue who
they thought to be John Ojahn
Two, their recently assigned
janitorial personnel from Unit Delta
6.

Taylor and Allen made their way towards the Unit's Central Core Chambers to retrieve the Lost Boys birth records among other information. Taylor and Lyman were communication experts and had monitored all High Command messages at will. It was how they were able to discover the existence of a mysterious virus that had been plaguing the System. Such virus had been the cause for the annihilation of several units. There was a failure to install an anti-virus.

It was during Clean-Up assignment when they were introduced to Janno, but as John. They had known enough through his odd behavior that he must have been assimilated prior to reassignment to their crew. Further reports intercepted had awakened their diminishing faith in old beliefs; the beliefs of Thunder Storm.

Knowledge of a group of rebels escaping from Unit Delta 6 had given them hope for freedom.

"How are we going to get him out?" Lyman asked.

"We'll explain that there was a mix up in fitness and that we are here to escort him back to Unit Beta 3." Rex answered.

"Do you think that will work?" Lyman asked.

"No" Rex confessed, "But something will come to me by the time we're ready to pull him out. You'll have to do the entire computer bypassing to get into the buildings. I had been counting on Gormely for that. Now I rely on you. Can you manage?"

"Piece of cake!" Lyman answered, "I wonder how Ruffer and Gormely are doing?"

CHAPTER TWENTY: SECTION ELEVEN PRISONERS

At sector Chi 7 quadrant 4, the Thunder Storm Warriors were preparing to ambush the incoming refuse transport shuttle. Peff called out the orders positioning his team were they would be most needed. "Alright you guys" Peff called out, "according to Luna, when I set off this frequency jamming device the truck will come to a complete halt. Astian will then switch on the transmitter device and attach it to the forepart of the truck. Orge and Arco will then board the shuttle. Are there any questions?" There were none. "Good! All we do now is sit tight and wait."

"I'm just about finished with the panel," Ruffer said.

"It's taking too long," Gormely said, "I'm not sure we'll be able to pull this off."

"We have to," Ruffer said, "We have no other choice. I'll grab on to your ankles and lower you down to the controls."

"Whatever you do," Gormely said, "Don't drop me!"

"All right!" Peff called out, "Here it comes! On my mark... now!" The shuttle stopped in its tracks. Gormley and Ruffer were flung out over the truck by the momentum. The awaiting party was taken by surprise. Peff called out for evasive action. "Stun weapons in effect!" he said.

But Arco had other ideas. "Stun weapons?" he said, "I'm a full armored Sentinel!" He jumped out of hiding and walked towards Ruffer and Gormely with laser aimed at them. "Identify yourselves!" He ordered.

"Omigosh! A Sentinel!" Ruffer exclaimed, "We have to get out of here! Run!"

"I can't!" Gormely yelled, "My leg is broken!"

"Surround them!" Peff called out. The warriors jumped out to form a circle around the two fallen men. Though Arco failed to follow orders as he seldom did every now and then, he had the right idea. "Identify yourselves!" Peff demanded.

"I am Ruffer Ojahn Two Six" Ruffer answered, "Clean-Up Crew Beta 1, Squad 3, Unit Beta 3.

"What about you shorty?" Arco asked.

"Shorty?!" Gormely protested, "I am Gormely Ojahn Seven, Commander! Clean-Up Crew Beta 1, Unit Beta 3!"

"Commander?" Ruffer questioned.

"Shhh!" Gormely ordered.

"What are you doing out here?" Orge asked removing his helmet.

"We got lost in navigation back to our unit," Gormely answered.

"A likely story!" Arco said.

"At ease!" Peff said, "Under the circumstances, we have to take you both prisoners. Yuan? Notify Luna. Tell her that we have some guests. And Astian? Contact Nica and inform her that we need her medical expertise. As for the rest of you, help turn this behemoth truck around so we can get going with our mission."

"In effect!" they hollered.

"Uh? Excuse me!" Ruffer said, "But you're just a bunch of Razzs. We're not on school grounds and have done you no wrong. You can't take us prisoners."

"I'm afraid we can, Sir" Peff said, "You're presence jeopardizes our freedom. Your companion has already tried to mislead us in calling himself a commander. All commanders' designations begin with Alpha and One. He tried to pass off his mischief with a designated Seven."

"But freedom is what we've been searching for" Ruffer said, "You don't understand. We've left some friends back at Unit Sigma 5, and we need to get them back."

"Sigma 5?" Peff questioned, "What do you know of Unit Sigma 5?"

"It's a medical station where Sentinels are made" Ruffer answered, "Where birth records are stored, where assimilation takes place. It is the weakest spot the system has, and an ideal place to attack if one wishes to free oneself from the system."

"Do you believe in Thunder?" Peff asked directly.

"I know of a violent storm" Ruffer answered.

CHAPTER TWENTY: SECTION TWELVE TO RESCUE JANNO

And back at Sigma 5: "Jeena?" Janno asked her, "Do you know where they have taken Dean Joan?"

"I lost sight of her shortly before I was brought in here" she answered, "But I believe they were taking her to a Master Assimila-thing. I really can't remember."

"Master Assimilation Monitor, where I was taken shortly before my transfer to Beta 3," Janno said, "Oh, by the way, I have been changing lately. I've gained the power to separate my spirit from my body and traverse through time and space."

"I believe you" Jeena said.

"You do?" He asked.

"Yes" she answered, "Cheynne was able to heal any wound with his touch."

"Cheynne?" Janno repeated, "Yes, I remember him. But what do you mean was?"

"He's dead" Jeena answered, "He was killed off by the High Command." A tear came to her eye. "His power for good was found evil by the High Command so he was eliminated." Janno stood silent for a moment.

"If there was some way of contacting Dean Joan," he said, "without the need to use my power, perhaps we could easily locate her exact whereabouts and rescue her. I don't want to set off any High Command alarms by using my power."

"Don't risk it" Jeena urged, "I couldn't bear it if anything should happen to you."

"I don't want anything happening to you either," Janno said, "Come, help me tie up these Sentries and then we'll find a way to locate Dean Joan."

After tying up the Sentries, Janno took hold of one of the Sentry's key access card to unlock the doors of the corridors they were in. "You're my prisoner, Ok, Jeena?" Janno said to her.

"Understood", she responded. Janno led her down the corridor to the admissions desk. He reported to the clerk behind the desk just as he would report to anyone were he undergoing Sentry duty back at Unit Delta 6 as the Sentry Number One. He continued escorting Jeena down the long corridor and when he was clear of the admissions desk's monitor:

"Jeena?" he told her, "To escape from the building I'm going to summon a bit of my energy and zap the door's lock. It won't be enough to cause alarm to the High Command, but just enough to get us out of here. This key card is no good. There is no magnet strip."

"Ok" she said, "Do it. I'm beginning to get scared." And as Janno used his power to bypass the magnetic lock of the outer doors to the Breeding Annex of the Solgi campus someone else was bypassing the locks from the outside to get in.

"Rex!" Janno called out.

"Keep it down, Razz!" Rex said. He took Janno by the collar and hauled him out of the building and Jeena along with him. "Let's get out of here!"

CHAPTER TWENTY
SECTION THIRTEEN: RALLY

And at the System's Recycling Center: "Thunder Storm Warriors, unite!" Luna had called out. Everyone from seniors to juniors rallied around her.

"Peff?!" she questioned, "Report status!"

"Scouts have left on truck to scope out Unit Sigma 5." Peff answered, "It is the nearest system unit to this center. They both have taken a modified copy of Jeppe's Squabble suit to merge in with Sentinels. Junior companion training held by Yuan are functioning accordingly. Strategic battle plans are on standby until the scout team returns. Debriefing procedures of our two prisoners: Complete."

"Satisfactory" Luna answered, "Medical?"

"Everyone passed their Physical Exam" Nica answered, "Except we won't have any supplies to take care of anyone if they should become seriously injured. We're using a splint to aid in Mr. Gormely's leg until Peff cam metamorphose again and heal him."

"No problem" Luna answered, "We'll just have to tough it out if the situation arises, at least until the boys get back hopefully with med supplies from Sigma 5. Weena? How goes the teachings?"

"The juniors understand full well the nature of the Most High" she answered, "They know, as well as we all do that without His help, we don't stand a chance."

"Good then" Luna reported, "I now relate the progress on the frequency shield. It is built. What remains are modification techniques which are currently being applied by Jeppe. Which leaves Queen and Alaetra?"

"We need everyone to suit up that we can modify any required alterations" Alaetra said.

"Not to mention the function of each suit" Queen added.

"It is good, then" Luna announced, "Until the scout teams returns, we shall be suiting up and learning how to use the armor. Thunder Storm; in effect!"

CHAPTER TWENTY ONE

SECTION ONE: ORPHANS

"We have no family" Taylor announced.

"What do you mean?" Allen asked.

"I can't get past our parents registry. The data has been corrupted as if someone yanked a device drive in a hurry to get scarced. It appears that each of us is an only child," Taylor answered, "Our parents were denied a second breeding process. The High Command tried to exterminate certain genes during a bottle neck effect of processing personnel. There's a slight chance that we might all be related pending the recovery of the data."

"Then we might be siblings to each other," Allen corrected, "What of our parents?"

"All were initialized," Taylor answered.

"Then they are dead and we're all on our own," Allen said.

"It matters not to me" Taylor said, "The Lost Boys have been like a family. Though the nuclear family has been dissolved by the Population Control Act of the High Command, corporate families do exist and at least we have each other to rely upon in times of distress."

"We had better meet up with Rex at the Master Assimilation Monitor and let him know what we have discovered in our birth records," Allen said, "Not to mention the other programs intercepted."

CHAPTER TWENTY ONE
SECTION TWO
TO RESCUE DEAN JOAN

Meanwhile at the Master Assimilation Monitor: Rex led Janno and Luna to the Annex while Lyman covered the rear. They had walked through the Outer System unquestioned. Had they been indoors perhaps their presence would have been under consideration but in the Outer System there were no monitors. The Outer System functioned perfectly according to the High Command. All business conducted there related solely to service of the High Command. Nothing else mattered there but the will of the system and it was why only initialized personnel were allowed to serve in this area. Having been initialized they would have no other purpose in existence other than to serve the system of the High Command. No supervision was needed as inside the building structures. Rex and his party were not questioned, simply because system servants were not consciously aware of them.

Moments later they bumped into Taylor and Allen. "Hey chief!" Allen said, "We've made it!"

"We're on time" Lyman agreed.

"Alright!" Rex exclaimed, "Our plan is working itself together!"

"You never specified why you wanted us to meet here," Taylor said.

"I had wanted to try and return Ruffer's and Gormely's psyches to them using the Master Assimilation Monitor," Rex said.

"How were you going to do that?" Lyman asked.

"By scanning for his specific coded brain waves, matching it up with what is stored within the assimilation monitor, then run the sequence in reverse" Rex answered.

"Simple logic!" Allen complimented.

"But weren't they assimilated back at Unit Beta 3?" Taylor questioned, "Shouldn't their psyches be logged on the Beta 3 Master Assimilation Monitor?"

"Technically, yes" Allen answered, "But the system is a

highly sophisticated computer network. What is stored in one memory bank can be accessed from any location throughout the system. We don't have to necessarily be back at Beta 3 to recover what we want."

"It doesn't make any difference," Lyman pointed out "Ruffer and Gormely are not here."

"Dean Joan!" Jeena announced.

"Dean who?" Taylor asked.

"Joan Ojahn Three from our Third Stage, Rendo Campus Institute at Beta 7," Rex answered.

"She's here?" Allen questioned.

"That's right and we have to bust her out!" Lyman answered.

"I can go in undetected," Janno said.

"How are you going to do that?" Taylor asked.

"I'm going to slip into a coma," Janno answered, "Then I will traverse the spectrum until I find her essence and virtually locate her within the computer's hard drive. I will her out of the Annex. Jeena will watch over my body."

"But wouldn't you alarm the High Command if you use your powers?" Jeena asked Janno.

"It's safe so as long I'm nowhere near any computer programs running," Janno answered, "Besides, we're in the Outer System. There's no need to be suspected"

"In that case, I'll watch over your body," Jeena said.

"That'll give us time to fill you in on what we've discovered," Allen told Rex.

"Slip into a coma?" Taylor questioned, "I'd better help you watch over him," he told Jeena.

Janno sat crossed leg. Jeena braced his back. A cool blue flame enveloped them then flew outward from Janno. {That wasn't so bad}, Janno thought, {It's beginning to hurt less and less. I think perhaps the gut wrenching pain must have had something to do with the presence of the High Command's software. Out in the Outer System there is nothing but walk ways and roads. It's meant for travel. I have to locate Dean Joan.} After a moment: {There she is, about to be assimilated. I know the experience. She is sedated. I can reach into her mind. Dean Joan! Dean Joan! Over here!}

{Huh?}, Dean Joan thought.

{Over here, Dean Joan} Janno thought to her, {Over here.}

{Janno?} she asked, {Janno Ojahn One? What are you doing here?}

{Dean Joan, I am here to rescue you} Janno thought, {You are undergoing assimilation process.}

{Is that what that yellow light beam is for?} she thought, {It's been causing me pain.}

{Then we must get out of here} Janno thought to her, {where pain will not follow.}

{And where is that?} She asked.

{Through the void of space} Janno answered.

{The void of space?} Joan questioned, {What exactly is the void of space and how did you get here?}

{Jeena Ojahn Six has told me that you are member to an underground society known as the Lost Boys but in your case: girl. You have beliefs that are exactly as the underground society I belong to. We are called Thunder Storm. In our beliefs there exists an event that we call Maturity or the Evolution. I believe that the Lost Boys referred to this event as the Mutation. I have mutated.

Our beliefs went along the lines as: throughout the

generations of time, because of the alpha brain wave stimulation brought to pass from the manipulation the High Command a day will come in which the brain would be enhanced enough to cause the human being to evolve into a state in where he has powers and abilities to do things he could not do before in an attempt to protect itself from such manipulation. Such enhancement begins with the eyes. In the past, a life time of television and monitor viewing has cause mankind's eye sight to become pixilated ergo evolution.

I could relate several examples to you but time does not permit. I have evolved. I have reached Maturity or have mutated. Whichever the case may be, I have gained powers and abilities that allow me transfer my spirit anywhere in time and space. I have met my parent, Joseph Adam Lezama. I am in his image. We both can perform similar talents. The difference is that he uses technology. I do not have to. I am bio-engineered.

I have left my body to come to your aid. I had been assimilated not too long ago. Thanks to Jeena, I have recovered myself. Being familiar with the assimilation sequence, I was able to locate your brain thought patterns and follow the transmission to you. It seems I got here in time.}

{Then, I'm not dreaming? Am I?} Joan thought, {I'm really being assimilated.}

{Yes. You are being assimilated} Janno thought, {And no, this is not a dream. Right now a group of friends await us outside the annex, but we must first survive the assimilation experience, and the only way to do that is to escape into the void of space.

The Pool of Thought is a place where all inspiration originates. Because of its immense force and sensation, the vibration frequencies are more than enough to keep us safe from the assimilating beam of the High Command. It is there where we will go.}

{In the void of space as you called it, can contact be made there with the dead?} Joan asked.

{I believe so, I've done it before. All we would have to do is peer through the veil} Janno answered. He waved a hand before him and time and space rolled over.

{Oh my God!} Joan exclaimed, {What is that?!}

{These are the dead} Janno answered.

{But they're all gray and motionless} Joan thought.

{It's because of the initialization process. These are the initialized servants of the system. They are half dead. Some who are totally dead are trapped in a state of confusion because they do not know that they are dead. Being surrounded by the Zombies gives cause for alarm. It is the total dead that I must reach and awaken them to a state of peace and awareness.}

{How are you planning to do that?} Joan asked.

{Simple} Janno answered, {I locate one who is completely dead and awaken him and he helps me find others to awaken and they help me find others, until we have formed a chain. For example Dean Joan, I have awakened Dean Troy} Janno opened the fabric of space.

{Troy!} Joan cried out in the astral plane.

{Hello Joan}, Troy answered with a smile. Joan moved towards him. She hugged him.

{I can feel you!} She thought.

{All spirit is matter} Troy thought back, {but such is more refined or more pure, and can only be seen by purer refined eyes.}

{Troy} Joan hugged him, then, {I'm sorry.}

{You have done nothing wrong, Joan.} Troy thought to her.

{I feel as though it were my fault that you were killed} she thought to him.

{Nonsense!} he thought, {No one is to blame except for the High Command.}

{Dean Troy?} Janno asked, {Have you been able to contact and alert the others?}

{See for yourself, Janno} Troy answered. And he rolled away the fabric of space as figures began to appear.

{Hello, Janno} Cheynne thought, {how goes the resistance?}

{Cheynne!} Janno thought, {you're awake!}

{I admit it took a while for me to understand what was going on} Cheynne confessed, {but I'm doing well. Allow me to introduce you to the rest of our team. This is Stick Shift.}, Cheynne thought.

{Hello} Stick Shift thought as he reached out to shake Janno's hand.

{He and I were killed personally by the High Command} Cheynne thought, {with him is Heide. She was terminated by a Sentinel. And so were Armie and her companion Meena. And finally we have Peps. Peps was terminated by a Digit Six.}

{You don' know how happy I am to see you all again} Janno thought.

{So am I}, Joan thought.

{We live in a quiet state} Troy thought, {but are confined to this astral plane unable to return into physical existence at least until the time of the Restoration to which Thunder Storm refers to as the Return.}

{What is it you do here?} Joan asked.

{We spend our time teaching the dead about who they are and where they came from} Cheynne answered, {And what awaits us at the time of the Return when our spirits will be tangible once again as with our bodies were, never to die again and we shall live in a state of perfection becoming immortals, and encompassed in a glory we do not yet know.}

{There are two others we would like you to meet, Janno} Troy thought to him.

{I'm Dino} thought a voice, {I was finished off by a Digit Six after a band of Sentries tore out my power unit when I functioned as a Sentinel.}

{And I hope you remember me} Mitro thought to Janno, {I was terminated by the same Digit Six while investigating a mute wave length at your recovery ward when I functioned as a Sentinel.}

{Mitro?!} Janno thought, {But I saw you hit with a laser by an invading Digit Six. Weren't you destroyed?}

{Janno, I was already half dead serving as a Sentinel. When the invading Digit Six shot me, it caused me to lose total control of my astral form and I reverted to my natural elements. The shock of death left me in such an unsettled state that I was among the Zombies until Troy found me.}

{Then Father was right} Janno thought, {There is no death only changes of state, shifts in dimensions.}

{That's right} Troy agreed.

{Uh, Janno, what Father?}, Cheynne asked.

{Oh, it was the voice!} Janno answered, {the voice I kept hearing when accessing my memories, when I originally gained entry way into the astral plane.} Janno answered, {Father guided me, through the process of maturity in which I gained the ability to separate my spirit from my body and enter into the void of space, traverse the spectrum, upgrade at the Pool of Thought, and much more. He came to me in the guise of a Counselor of the High Command for my benefit.}

{Oh} Cheynne thought.

{We have established an order} Stick Shift thought, {It was necessary to further the work of relaying Thunder Storm beliefs to the inanimate and have them become aware of the state they are in. Dean Troy has been elected to be our president.}

{That's an awesome idea} Janno thought, {the teaching of our beliefs requires organization and good leadership.}

{I don't do the work alone} Troy thought, {I have two Counselors.}

{Counselors?} Janno thought.

{Yes} Troy thought back, {Cheynne and Mitro are my counselors. They not only help me alert the total dead to existence, but they also help me organize a battle plan against the invasion of High Command.}

{I have had my suspicions about the infiltration of the universe by the High Command} Janno thought, {I'll have you know that this part is cordoned off by four pyramid satellites vibrating at this same frequency. That leaves the High Command oblivious to the existence of the remaining realm, but leaves you trap here as well.}

{What do you mean?} Stick Shift asked.

{I call them three dimensional trapezoid-like

constructions} Janno thought, {They can take you to any part of the cosmos you wish to explore. But because I witness a Digit Six in its astral form wearing full body armor, I concluded that it wouldn't be long before the manipulating brain waves of the High Command fine tunes itself into the astral plane and hold it captive as it does the physical realm.

I therefore had to find a way to stop this by creating eight laser pyramids and positioning them and the boundaries of the Pool of Thought and the Veil. Existence here is a cube encircling the planet.}

{That was very strategic} Mitro thought, {I was hoping there would be more to this astral plane than just the Pool of Thought.}

{There is} Janno thought, {But none can cross over but me.}

{How's that?} Stick Shift asked.

{I have the vibration frequency code stored within a pyramid near the veil at the void in space} Janno answered. {I had to pull out the external hard drive from its connection inappropriately as I was in a rush and so I inadvertently deleted irrelevant data or else I had gone for another drive before Jeena and I reunited with the Los Boys.

CHAPTER TWENTY ONE
SECTION THREE: THE TUB FACILITIES

Meanwhile outside the Assimilation Annex: "They need to be destroyed," Allen said, "The Tub facilities are as inhumane now as they were before."

"We were watching the procedure" Taylor said, "Apparently something is wrong, because seven out of ten infants drown each time they're dropped into the Tub."

"That shouldn't be happening" Allen said, "Normally, one in fifteen drowns. At least that's how the current statistics show. But what we witness was something else."

"I suspect that due to the virus which has been infecting the system, compatible gene selections can't be made. Furthermore the babies are being born deformed" Rex announced, "Brain hemorrhage occurs and there seems to be no natural cause."

"That accounts for poor performance at the Tub" Lyman added.

"If too many children are drowning in the process to make Sentinels, then we have to find a way to stop it." Rex said.

"Easier said than done" Allen said, "It'll be difficult to blow up the tub facilities without endangering the lives of the new born babies."

"Perhaps we can stop the program using a computer bypass code." Taylor suggested.

"That may work better than destroying the facilities, at least until the babies are cleared from them." Rex agreed.

"There's only one problem" Allen pointed out.

"What's that?" Lyman asked.

"Who will care for them? And we'll still have to access the

Central Core Chambers." Allen responded. Just then two black armored Sentinels appeared.

<Personnel identify!> commanded the voice.

"Oh no!" Taylor said, "We're in for it!"

"We're not prepared for this" Rex admitted. A blue light appeared above their heads. It phased through the two Sentinels. The light returned to Janno and he came to.

"Are you alright?" Jeena asked him.

"I'm fine" he answered, "But I think we're in trouble. I tried to use my power to disrupt the frequency in the Sentinels hoping to short circuit something but nothing seemed to work. Spirit has an electrical charge, positive or negative. I don't know what went wrong."

<Nothing's gonna work on us> said the first Sentinel removing his helmet. We're not machines." It was Arco. "Orge is in the other suit" he said.

"What gives Janno, man?"

"Arco?!" Janno asked.

"In the flesh." he answered.

"You know him?" Rex inquired.

"We were team mates in Squabble." Janno said getting up from the floor where he sat. Jeena rose up with him.

<Leave it to Janno to be in the arms of a lovely girl while the rest of us battle the System> Orge

announced, <You had better put your helmet on Arco, we don't know who's watching us.> Arco placed his helmet back on.

<I know the look on your faces> Arco said, <But it's a long story. We were sent to scout out the perimeters but we caught a couple of your guys who informed us about your proceedings>

"A couple of our guys?" Taylor questioned.

<Ruffer and Gormely> Orge said.

"Ruffer and Gormely?" Allen asked, "They're Ok?"

<They're safe with us back at our camp site at Sector Chi 7, Quadrant 4> Orge said, <We're to escort you back to the site once we've made contact>

"That's going to be a little bit difficult to do," Lyman said, "We have other plans."

<Oh?> Arco said.

"Dean Joan will be escorted out shortly by real Sentinels" Janno said, "We have to cut her loose and neutralize the Assimilation Monitor."

"Neutralize the Monitors?" Rex questioned.

"Actually, I meant destroy them" Janno said, "With the Assimilation Monitor destroyed, all memories, thoughts, and ideas, stored within the banks will filter through into the astral plane's Pool of Thought and return to its proper owner."

"You mean Ruffer and Gormely will recover their memories?" Lyman asked.

"I think not," Allen answered, "They were assimilated back at Beta 3."

"It might work if we establish a link between all the system's assimilation monitors to have them disrupt in sequence," Janno said.

"But for that we would have to go to the Central Core Chambers," Taylor said, "and access it from there."

"Well, we now have two reasons to go to the Central Core Chambers" Rex said, "only not everybody needs to go."

"I'm the only one qualified to establish a computer link up

between monitors," Taylor said, "I should be the one to go."

"And I lead this crew" Rex announced, "So, that means I get to go along. The rest of you head back to Sector Chi 7, Quadrant 4. When we're through we'll meet you there."

"That's if you survive!" Lyman pointed out.

<There's no need to place your selves at risk> Orge said through his helmet, <We have assembled a group of warriors who wait to attack Sigma 5 after we get in touch with them. We could all head back to Sector Chi 7, Quadrant 4 after rescuing Dean Joan and regroup to return in full force. There doesn't have to be any risk involve>

"It sounds like a better plan" Allen said.

"I admit that it is so" Rex agreed, "Let's do it that way." They awaited Dean Joan's transfer return from the Assimilation Annex. She was being escorted out by two Sentinels that were intercepted by laser blasts from Arco and Orge.

The small team stood at alert aware that any danger could come from any direction. They took hold of Dean Joan and scrambled for the outer perimeters of Sigma 5 where the confiscated refuse transport shuttle awaited them. They had no trouble boarding the vehicle and in no time they were on their way back to Sector Chi 7, Quadrant 4; the Recycling Center.

CHAPTER TWENTY ONE
SECTION FOUR: SENTINEL
ALPHA 3 MARK 215

The chamber door slid open and the icy mist flowed from within. Digit Six was kept in suspended animation at all times. This particular unit was strictly for defensive purposes and activated solely under emergency situations. Its armor was red. There was nothing human about a Digit Six. Whatever humanity, it may have had, was taken long ago during Initiation Sequence.

<Sigma 5 Digit One this is Sentinel Alpha 3 Mark 215, over>

<Digit Six: this is Digit One, come in, over>

<Missing sentinels recovered. Elements: defunct. 10-20 Assimilation Annex. Terrorist activity

suspected.   Converting: search mode, in effect, over>

    <Digit Six, locate terrorists: transfer to Sigma 5 Central Core Chambers for High Command Central Core Chamber transport, over>

    <Roger that: Digit One. This is Digit Six Alpha 3 Mark 215, out!> The Sentinel was unleashed.   It strode forth with only one objective recognized. Unlike other Sentinels, who had to request certain access codes to carry out their duties, a Digit Six did not have such limits. <Applying thermal infra red scanners> said the Digit Six. It sought the area surveying the damage done to the two Sentinels using specialized lenses adapted into its visors. <Armored padded boot prints detected.   Seven distinct boot prints detected. Prints: leading to Refuse Transport

Shuttle Bay. Digit Six in tracking mode ...tracking... tracking... tracking...>

The Sentinel followed the foot prints to the shuttle bay where the prints ended and new evidence was discovered. <Surveying area> said the Digit Six, <Prints come to a halt. Shuttle tire marks begin. Adapting: magnifying visors. Magnify 40 x 10 ^{100} : Scanning horizon> The Sentinel surveyed the landscape and far from a distance it spotted the escaping refuse transport shuttle. <Digit Six to Sigma 5 Division Factor Alpha 3 Squad 1, Squad 1 activate!> came the order.

All around the Sigma 5's Central Core Chambers, cylinder doors slid open and icy mist flowed without. The Sentinels came to life receiving transmissions into their helmets.

They formed into a squad and marched towards the Refuse Transport Shuttle Bay where their commander the Digit Six Alpha 3 Mark 215 awaited them. Then came the remaining order: <Squad 1 in pursuit mode!> said the Digit Six.

<In effect!> came the response.

CHAPTER TWENTY TWO

SECTION ONE: FIRST KISS

"I'm finished" Jeppe announced.

"Good!" Luna said and threw herself on him, kissing him.

"Luna?! Luna?! Wait!! Stop!! I'm not finished!"

"What is it now?" she asked him.

"We have to test out this radar jamming device" he answered.

"Well, it should work should it not?" she questioned.

"Perhaps we should turn it on" he said.

"What if it doesn't work?" she asked him.

"Then I'll blame it on you" he answered.

"On me?!" she questioned.

"Yes, you!" he said taking her by the waist and dipping her into a kiss.

"Whoa!" she exclaimed, "I thought you didn't know how to kiss?"

"I fibbed. Now, let's get this contraption running" he said, "I've been working on it for hours." He pulled the switch. For a moment nothing happened, suddenly the vibrations came. It was triangular in shape, very much like a pyramid. A beam shot out from the top and spread out through the air encasing the quadrant within a thin film of light forming a dome. "I wonder how far it stretches." Jeppe asked, "We should measure it to have everyone under its protection."

"I'll have guards posted at its perimeters" Luna said, "Once we've located them, that is. The force field will keep out all frequencies sent out by the High Command. Any equipment we want to use will have to undergo modification techniques. We'll have to adapt them to function without codes."

"I agree" Jeppe said, "All we have is this one generator we've put together. We need other sources of power. Perhaps solar powered generators can be built?"

"Queen and Alaetra are working on that" Luna said, "Ace is giving them a hand. The junior companions are in full body armor and are available to help us measure the force field. Only, we'll need more scanners."

"We can modify the visual receptors to scan for energy" Jeppe said.

"That sounds like a good idea" Luna said, "Let's get moving."

CHAPTER TWENTY TWO
SECTION TWO: PURSUIT

Far away from the sector: <Don't look now, but we're being followed!> Arco hollered. All heads within the shuttle turned. On the horizon, they saw them coming in a small swarm.

"What are those?!" Allen asked.

"They're Sentinel Personnel Carriers!" Janno answered, "Coded SPC. I inspected one once when I was the Sentry Number One at Delta 6."

"How many are there?" Rex asked.

<I count, eleven!> Orge answered.

"What are our assets?" Janno inquired.

"We have two laser-rifles we took from the Sentinels at the Assimilation Annex" Taylor answered.

<And two more lasers built into our armors> Arco said, <We can take on any Sentinel one on one>

"The rest of us won't be much use and will stand as helpless targets, but perhaps we can even the odds. Orge, move over! I'm driving!" Janno said. They scrambled for position. "How fast can this thing go?" Janno asked.

<Not fast enough!> Orge answered, <I'll climb up top to get a bearing on our pursuers. I can target some of them>

<I'll give you a hand!> Arco said.

"We'll cover the rear!" Lyman said.

"Refuse Transport Shuttles aren't meant for speed" Allen said, "Maybe we can change that."

"How are you going to get to the engine from the inside?" Rex asked.

"We can re-wire the energy output rotating the wheels from the inside," Allen answered.

"Oh" Taylor said. The small crew began to prepare for the confrontation up ahead. Janno drove. Orge and Arco were up on the cab. Lyman and Rex covered the rear. Allen and Taylor worked at the cab's inside panels. Jeena and Joan held on tightly to each other.

The desert terrain vibrated. The horizon shook. The squad of Sentinels closed in on the shuttle. <They're gaining on us!> Arco called out.

<You have to speed up, Janno!> Orge yelled.

"I'm going as fast as I can!" Janno yelled back, "Taylor! I need more power!"

"We're to the max, Razz!" Taylor called out.

"Then hang on!" Janno yelled, "I'm going to maneuver us through!" A laser shot down at the vehicle missing it by seconds.

<That was close!> Orge yelled.

<Shoot back!> Arco yelled out, <Shoot back!>

<They're moving around too fast!> Orge said.

<Use a controlled burst of rapid fire!> Arco called out.

<I got one! I got one!> Orge exclaimed.

<Oooh! It just smashed into a second one!> Arco yelled.

"Those Razzs think we're playing a game!" Lyman told Rex.

"Whatever it may be to them, they seem to have the right idea" Rex said, "Use a controlled burst of rapid fire."

"Hang on! We're swerving!" Janno yelled. The lasers came.

Janno anticipated the shots. He maneuvered as best as he could but he could not anticipate every shot. The vehicle was hit. "We're hit! We're hit!" Janno yelled out. The passenger door blew open. The vehicle hit a dune. The cab bounced. Allen fell near the door way.

"I've got you! I've got you!" Taylor yelled.

"Whatever you do don't let go!" Allen yelled back.

"Hang on! I gotta swerve!" Janno hollered.

"No!" Taylor yelled, "We'll lose him!"

<We're gonna get hit!> Orge hollered.

"I've got him! Swerve!" Taylor yelled. Janno turned the vehicle in time to miss another hit from the pursuing lasers. He step on the accelerator and weaved his way through the sand.

"I'm back on track!" Janno yelled out, "We may get out of this one yet!" But Janno spoke too soon. A laser shot into the front left wheel. "I'm losing it!" he yelled, "I'm losing it!" The vehicle overturned. "Hang on!" Janno yelled, "This is going to hurt." The vehicle tumbled over and over again. It rolled ten feet and came to a dead stop. Dust flew out into the air. The Sentinels were closing in.

<Aaaggghhh!>, Arco yelled, <Gotta get this sand off of me! Orge?! Orge?! Where are you?!>

<I'm here! I'm here!> Orge answered.

<Dig yourself a position!> Arco called out, <Sentinels: coming in!>

"Jeena?! Jeena?!" Janno called out as he scrambled out of the sand.

"I'm over here!" Jeena called back, "Dean Joan is hurt. I've got to help her."

"Roll call, in effect!" Rex hollered.

"Lyman, in effect!" he yelled.

"Allen, in effect!" he yelled. Then there was silence. The cloud of dust was settling down.

"Taylor?!" Rex called out to him, "Taylor?!"

"I've found him!" Allen yelled, "I've found him! He's not moving!"

225

"Check his vitals!" Rex ordered, scrambling to reach them.

"I'm not getting anything!" Allen said, "He's got no pulse! He's got no pulse! No air! No air! He's not breathing! He's not breathing! "

"CPR: in effect!" Rex called out joining Allen. He positioned himself over Taylor's head trading places with Allen. "One! Two! Push! Push! Push! Push! Push! Repeat the cycle! One! Two! Push…!"

"We're losing him!" Allen said, "We're losing him!"

"Shut up!" Rex yelled, "We're not losing him! We're not losing him! Repeat the cycle! One! Two! Push!"

<Sentinels, on line!> Orge called out. The Sentinel came to a stand up top on its pursuit carrier. It was a mistake. Arco had him dead on sight.

<Got him!>, boasted Arco. Orge shot the next Sentinel and it crashed its pursuit carrier onto another. <You got another two for one, Orge!> Arco yelled. Lyman shot the next Sentinel. <Hey! We just might win this one!> Arco said as he shot his laser back into the line of Sentinels.

<Squad 1, Factor 3, secure site> ordered the Digit Six. <Locate any survivors and neutralize>

"There's five of them left!" Lyman said, "We fight or die!"

<Never say die!> Arco hollered.

"Jeena? Dean Joan?" Janno called to them, "Stay under cover until we call for you."

"One! Two! Push! Push! Push...!" Rex continued.

"He's gone, chief!" Allen yelled, "He's gone!" Rex stopped the CPR procedures. He banged his fist onto Taylor's chest. It was useless to do so. Taylor was dead. Rex was filled with rage. He picked up his laser rifle and stepped out to face the Sentinels. Arco and Orge had dug out positions for themselves at the rear of the crash site. Lyman covered them from above as he was up atop the shuttle.

The Sentinels converged around the crash site. They took out Lyman easily. He couldn't move much. He had a broken leg. He failed to dodge the blast from the Sentinel's armament. Janno went to him. He took the laser rifle from his hands and waited the incoming sentinels. Arco held his ground firing and shielding the blasts shot back at him. Orge was standing his ground as well. Rex buried himself beneath the sand to camouflage himself with his surroundings. He shot back at the Sentinels. He scuttled through the sand hoping to gain a better position crawling to the forepart of the crash site. As he crawled through his hand hit an armored padded boot. It was white.

<Hey, Mister?!> Jeppe called out, <What are you doing down in the sand?> Rex looked up. He wasn't sure what to make of the situation. The white armored sentinel standing before him was too small to be a Sentinel.

"You a Digit One?" Rex asked.

<A Digit One?! Nonsense!> he answered, <I am Jeppe, Unit Commander, Team Alpha Three! We're here to rescue you. Standby while I signal to the other teams> Jeppe raised his hands over his head and waved them across the air before him. <Team leader three to Team leader one, we're in position, over>

<This is team leader one> Peff said, <Standby, on my mark prepare to attack!>

"We're surrounded!" Janno cried out.

<We're being pinned down!> Arco yelled, <Can't get clear!>

<Alpha Team One!> Peff called out, <Into battle!> They sprung out from the dunes behind

the crashed vehicle firing their laser in all different directions. Two sentinels were struck and short circuited to their end. <Alpha Team Two!> Peff called out, <Attack!>

The second wave of rebels jumped out from their hiding places to fire their lasers at the remaining sentinels. All fell but one. The Digit Six remained alert. "We got a Digit Six before us!" Janno yelled out, "Concentrate your fire in the same location; behind the head plate!" Arco shot his laser. Orge followed. Then Janno shot his and the Digit Six fell losing its helmet as it dropped to the ground. The human head was exposed and Janno could identify the figure that had been hunting them down. "Gasto!!" he yelled.

<What?> Arco yelled back.

<We just killed off Gasto!>
Orge said removing his helmet, "I
don't believe it."

"He was already dead" Janno
said, "We just freed his soul. He
was my kin from a different father."
Jeppe removed his helmet.

"Janno! Janno!" he called
out. He ran towards him.

"Jeppe?" Janno asked, "Is that
you?"

"It sure is, Senior" Jeppe
answered.

"How did you get down here?"
Janno asked.

"We hopped an RTS" Jeppe
answered, "We're in the middle of
the desert, the perimeters of Sector
Chi 7, Quadrant 4, the recycling
center. We were checking out the

distance of the field platform's screening when we saw you coming. We couldn't attack due to the limited range of our fire arms and had to wait until you were in such range."

"Are we at the Recycling Center?" Janno asked.

"As far as I can tell, Senior" Jeppe replied.

"Somebody help me with Lyman!" Rex called out.

"Arco? Orge?" Janno called out.

"In effect, chief!" they answered.

<Whoa! What's going on here?> Peff asked. He took off his helmet. "We have a chain of

command and it needs to be adhered to!"

"Who's in charge here?" Rex asked.

"I am, for now!" Peff answered.

"I need help with my friend" Rex said, "He's been hurt."

"I can take care of him," Peff said, "But first we have to secure the area. Team leaders Two and Three, secure the area! Team one: assist with injured personnel." Peff walked over to Rex and Lyman.

"What are you going to do to him?" Rex asked.

"Do you believe in Thunder?" Peff asked.

"I know of a violent Storm" Rex answered.

"I have Matured and can channel healing energy through my hands. I'm going to place my hands on top of his leg and heal his injuries. I'm about to metamorphose." Peff placed his hands upon Lyman's leg. There was a bright glow. Lyman's leg was made whole again.

"Unbelievable!" Rex remarked.

"No, not really," Peff answered, "Not when you understand the energy that encompasses and links mankind together." Not only was Lyman healed but the most remarkable thing happened: Taylor came back to life.

"Team Leader One!" Ace yelled out, "Area is secured."

"Roger that: team leader two!" Peff said, "Alright everyone! Listen up! Team One, grab your injured and let's head back to camp. Team Two, close up the rear. Team Three, you're on perimeter watch! Stay within the zone! Report anything unusual!"

They were well disciplined and they took their orders from one person. That person was Peff. Luna was back in the recycling center watching over Fatima. They picked up their belongings and marched out the area. "Welcome to the Junk Yard!" Peff told Janno.

"I'm happy to be here" Janno said, "Hey? How did you do that back there?"

"Uh, with Lyman?" Peff asked.

"Yeah, with Lyman and Taylor?" Janno answered.

"It took me a while to get use to it, but I somehow managed to control it", Peff said, "The metamorphoses acts with an adrenaline surge. In the heat of battle it manifests. However, I can induce it whenever I need to simply by causing my heart beat to race."

"Sounds like you're in control" Janno said, "Can you do something for Dean Joan? She doesn't look so hot."

"Where is she?" Peff asked.

"Jeena has her," Janno answered.

Peff walked to Jeena. He looked over Dean Joan. She was dehydrated. Peff placed his

237

hands upon her head and in a few moments she was well.   "That'll help you until we reach our camp site," Peff said.

Arco and Orge walked with Taylor.   Allen too walked beside them. Rex walked in front of them. He was deep in thought.   Taylor had just died but that did not bother him for long.   After witnessing the healing performed on Lyman and Taylor's revival, he knew with a conviction that the rest of the tales concerning the Lost Boys were true.   The existence of the astral plane was real. Restoration was true. Mutation was possible. All this was fascinating to Rex.   He viewed the armored personnel around him marching towards camp. Freedom existed.

At the perimeters of Sector Chi 7, Quadrant 4 Jeppe took charge of insuring that the quadrant stayed secure. He removed his helmet. "Alright team" he said, "position the screen receptors in their proper location. It won't be long before the sun goes down. We need to stay up and alert in case anything happens. Vikki: you're with Angie. Deena: you're with Tina. Luani: you're with Litra. That leaves Lisa with Sajie. Patrol your respective sectors around the perimeter and report in every session to me. We've got the front line to secure tonight. Team two has the rear post. Any questions: contact me via your helmet transmitters.

These are you radio codes: Vikki and Angie: you're Team Three Alpha Two. Deena and Tina: you're Alpha Three. Luani and Litra: you're Omega One. Lisa and Sajie: that leaves you with Omega Two. I'm to be address as Alpha

One. Alright, report to your sectors!"

"In effect!" they responded.

CHAPTER TWENTY TWO
SECTION THREE: C SECTION

Meanwhile en route to the camp site: "How long have you been out here?" Janno asked.

"This will be our second night" Peff responded.

"Second night?" Janno questioned, "I saw you in the astral plane about three nights ago."

"I remember" Peff said, "You warned me about Sentinels converging upon the Health Annex back at Delta Six. How did you do that?"

"I was already in the astral plane" Janno answered, "It was you who reached me. My guess is that prior to Maturity, we all make a quick stop in the astral plane."

"You could be right" Peff said, "I haven't been able to do that since."

"Peff! Peff!" Luna cried out, "I need your help."

"What's wrong?" Peff asked, "What is it?"

"Fatima is having contractions!" Luna cried, "Her baby is coming!"

"Team Two Omega One and Two: Nica and Vette!" Peff called out, "Report to the infirmary, on the double!"

They came running as fast as they could, stripping off their armor. "Oh, I knew they should have stayed behind!" Luna said.

"Are you not qualified to assist in the matter?" Janno asked.

"I'm classified 6-A" Luna responded, "Unless she was a machine there's nothing I can do."

"We're here!" Nica said, "Where is she?"

"She's inside the tent" Luna answered.

"It's Ok, we'll take care of her" Vette said.

"Oh no! We have a problem in here!" Nica yelled.

"What is it?" Vette asked.

"Her water just broke!" Nica answered, "And she hasn't dilated enough!"

"You'll have to cut her open," Janno yelled from outside the tent.

"We can't do that!" Vette yelled.

"Why not?" Luna asked.

"We don't know how to!" Nica answered, "We've never gone that far in our 3-A sessions."

"We need to get that baby out of her fast!" Janno said, "Or it could die."

"Aren't you a 1-B student?" Luna asked.

"He's versed in all fields," Peff answered.

"I'll need a laser," Janno said.

"Team Two Alpha Two: Alaetra, Queen?" Peff called out, "I need an independent laser at the infirmary!" Queen and Alaetra came running bringing the hand held laser requested. A small crowd gathered outside the tent.

"I'm going in!" Janno said, "Peff?! You'll have to come with me. We'll need your healing ability."

"You've got it!" Peff said.

"We need to wash up first," Janno said. Peff stripped off his armor.

"Over here!" Luna called out, "There's water in this barrel. It's not for drinking, so it will have to do." Janno washed up then grabbed the laser and went into the tent.

He unzipped his uniform to waist line and removed his T-shirt wrapping it around his mouth and nose. The mouth is the most germ area of the body. To deliver a child free from the contamination of germs, the mouth must be covered. Peff washed up behind him.

"Ok, Fatima" Janno said, "This is going to burn a bit." Janno concentrated the laser to cut across her abdomen. "Nica, Vette, hold her steady."

"Omigod! It burns!" Fatima cried out.

"Hang on!" Vette cried.

"Ok, I've got the baby" Janno said, "Oh no! It's not breathing."

"Give it to me. I know infant CPR," Nica said. Janno gave her the baby. He could have done it himself but he was more concerned with keeping Fatima's abdomen together. The baby cried. It was alive. Janno use the laser on the umbilical cord. Just then Peff walked in.

"What do I do?" he asked.

"Apply your healing touch to her abdomen" Janno said. Peff went to Fatima. He placed his hands upon her stomach and began to glow. In minutes, Fatima was made whole.

"That took longer than I thought," Peff said, "I'm drained!" He tried to rise but his knees gave way and he fell back. Janno went to him.

"Easy, Peff, I've got you" Janno said. He began to glow. His light rejuvenated Peff.

"How did you do that?" Peff asked.

"I don't know," Janno confessed, "It just happened."

"The baby is so cute!" Vette said wrapping the baby up in aluminum foil.

"Congratulations, Fatima!" Nica said, "You've just given birth to a healthy baby boy!" Fatima began to cry.

"What's wrong?" Vette asked.

"I want Sebb!!" Fatima cried out.

CHAPTER TWENTY THREE

SECTION ONE: PERIMETER DUTY

<Team Two Alpha One to Team Two!> Ace said through his helmet, <Let's pick up these screen receptors and get moving. We have perimeter duty at the rear. Team Two Omega One and Two: you're being reassigned. Nette: you're with Betty and are now Omega One. Nica: you're with Vette and are now Omega Two. Omega Two: you're staying behind to watch over Fatima and the new born. Everyone else, let's move out!>

CHAPTER TWENTY THREE
SECTION TWO: BABY SEBB

Inside the tent: "What are you going to call him?" Vette asked.

"I'm going to name him after his father, Sebb." Fatima answered.

"Sebb?" Nica asked, "Wasn't he shot down at the Health Annex?" Fatima began to cry. "Oh no, no, don't cry!" Nica said, "I'm sorry, I didn't mean to bring it up. Here, here, look at baby Sebb." Fatima's tears subsided.

"He's beautiful!" Fatima said, "He has his father's eyes." She sniffled.

"Oh, girl, I'm so happy for you!" Vette said.

CHAPTER TWENTY THREE
SECTION THREE: THE TUB TEST

Outside the tent: "I say we give the Razz the tub test" Arlos said.

"That's ridiculous!" Astian said, "He doesn't belong to us!"

"That's Sebb's Razz," Arlos said, "Sebb was a Rank One Sentry. His son deserves to be initiated into the rank of Sentries."

"What if he drowns?" Yuan asked.

"He won't drown!" Arlos continued, "If it doesn't seem that he will swim to the surface, one of us can pull him out."

"That'll bring shame upon the baby." Astian said.

"Who will train it, then?" Yuan questioned.

"There's no shame in helping the baby reach the surface" Arlos said.

"What's going on here?" Arco asked.

"Arlos wants to throw the baby into the Tub" Yuan answered.

"Hey? That's a good idea!" Arco said, "I'll get the barrel."

"Wait a minute, Arco!" Orge cut in, "You're not going anywhere."

"Aw, come on!" Arco pleaded, "This is our chance to continue with our traditions and our Code of Honor."

"Sebb would have wanted it this way" Arlos said.

"That's all understandable" Orge said, "But I believe that there are some people that won't agree with our ideas."

"Then we'll just have to rub them out!" Arco Razzded, gesturing as if he had lasers.

"Guys?" Yuan called out, "I don't feel so hot!"

Yuan clutched on to his stomach and fell back. He broke out in a sweat. "Call Peff!" Orge directed.

"Peff!" Astian yelled out.

In moments, Peff came running. With him was Janno. "What is it?" Peff inquired.

"Something's wrong with Yuan" Astian answered.

"I'm the Unit Commander for Team One, not the medic!" Peff told him.

"It's Ok", Janno said, "I know what's going on with him. He's Mutating. Help me get him into the infirmary. He just needs to rest."

"I'll carry him" Arco said picking Yuan up. He strode towards the camp's infirmary to where he laid Yuan upon a cot. The infirmary was composed of tents made out of canvass that were found lying around the center. Water was supplied by an old existing plumbing system. The water was not good for drinking at first, and so was therefore boiled. The renegade army had made for themselves suitable living conditions.

"What's going on now?" Nica asked Peff.

"It's Yuan" Peff answered, "He needs rest."

"Nette had related to us that he would be changing soon" Vette said.

"Is that why he was examined so many times?" Nica asked.

"Well I hope he's up and about soon" Peff said, "There's a lot to prepare for."

"I think we should stay with Yuan a while, Peff." Janno said, "It'll be his first time in the astral plane and that could shake him up a bit."

"What do you suggest we do?" Peff asked.

"I'm going detach my spirit from my body and venture into the astral plane." Janno said, "I need you to watch over my body."

"I see no problem with that" Peff said.

"What are you guys up to?" Vette inquired.

"Nothing, Vette" Peff said, "Please keep an eye on Fatima. We'll take care of Yuan."

"If you insist, boss man," Vette said. Janno sat crossed leg at the foot of Yuan's cot. Peff joined him. They closed their eyes. In a moment a cool blue flame enveloped Janno. Then it encircled Peff. It hovered above Yuan and then disappeared.

{What are you doing here?} Janno thought.

{I don't know} Peff confessed, {I'm supposed to be looking over your body.}

{Well, it doesn't matter} Janno thought, {you can help me locate Yuan. Look! Over there: a road.}

{It leads in all different directions} Peff thought, {what is it?}

{It is the large and spacious road} Janno responded, {It's where Yuan's thought patterns lead. He's lost. Let's float!}

{Float?} Peff inquired.

{We're in a realm where the laws of physics do not apply} Janno thought, {Here thought is energy and can be shaped into anything. We can fly.}

{Oh} Peff thought.

They took to the air floating above the dreary road following its course.　　{There's something coming in our direction} Janno thought.

{It looks like people} Peff thought.

{No! Wait! They're not people} Janno thought, {they're the walking dead.}

{Zombies?!} Peff thought.

{Exactly!} Janno thought, {they're being controlled by the High Command's frequencies. If they see us they'll extinguish our life force and we might become like them. We have to hide.}

{Where?} Peff asked.

{Over here, behind the veil} They ascended high above the lone and dreary road covering themselves behind the veil.

{Look, down there!} Peff thought, {they have Yuan captured.} Janno looked closely. It wasn't Yuan they had prisoner.}

{That's not Yuan} Janno thought, {that's Sebb!}

{Sebb?} Peff thought, {Well, it doesn't matter. We still have to rescue him.}

{Hold it!} Peff thought, {something's quite not right here.}

{What do you mean?} Peff asked.

{In my last visit to the astral plane} Janno answered, {I met a group of people that have all died whose spirit bodies now inhabit the astral plane. Sebb wasn't among that group.}

{He should have been} Peff thought, {Sebb was shot down at a small fire fight we had engaged ourselves in, back at Delta 6.}

{Oh, I wasn't sure wether he were dead or not} Janno thought.

{Perhaps he was taken prisoner before he could reach the group} Peff thought.

{You have a point} Janno thought, {Get ready to rescue him. On my mark, we'll rush down and pull him up into the veil.}

{Won't we be seen?} Peff asked.

{We'll be traveling at the speed of light} Janno said, {All you have to do is think it. Standby, one...two...three! }. Just as they planned, they so acted. The zombies did not have a clue as to what had happen. They simply observed Sebb disappear from their sights. They thought it insignificant to lose their prisoner. They continued their march. Zombies weren't much for brains.

{What the-?} Sebb thought.

{Easy, Sebb, we've got you} Peff thought.

{Peff, Janno?!} Sebb asked, {How did you guys get here?}

{We've Matured} Janno answered.

{How about you?} Peff asked, {How did you get caught by those Zombies?}

{I was running covert operations after being awakened by Dean Troy} Sebb replied, {The High Command's frequencies bombarded the astral plane two sessions ago. I was behind enemy lines within the cordoned off cube when it happened. I couldn't reach the others in time to warn them about the Zombie march. I was swept away without warning myself.}

{Where were they taking you to?} Janno asked.

{I was blinded by the High Command frequencies the entire time until now} Sebb answered.

{That's not much help} Peff thought.

{We'll have to get out of here soon} Janno thought.

{Where to?} Sebb asked, {The Zombies have control over most of the sector.}

{We're going to a place they can't follow.} Janno said, {we're going into Eternity, behind the veil through the void of space. Follow me!} In moments they reached their destination.

{What do we do here?} Peff asked.

{We visualize a doorway} Janno answered.

{Look!} Sebb thought, {There it is!} They went to the doorway. Janno gave three knocks.

{Who goes there?}, asked a voice.

{It is Janno and his companions} Janno answered.

{What is wanted?} asked the voice.

{We desire passageway into Eternity} Janno answered.

{Step before the doorway and receive the sign} said the voice. Janno stepped before the doorway and received the sign. {What is this?} asked the voice.

{The token of brotherhood} Janno answered.

{Give us the password} said the voice.

{The word is Thunder Storm} Janno thought.

{That is correct} said the voice, {you may enter.} The doorway was opened. Janno and his companions stepped through.

{Cheynne?!} Janno thought.

{You're the voice?} Peff asked.

{It was my shift} Cheynne answered.

{So, this is Eternity, huh?} Sebb remarked.

{It's where time stands still} Cheynne responded, {I'm glad to see that you've made it back, Sebb.}

{No thanks to you guys!} Sebb thought.

{We waited for you to return to us from you reconnaissance. We saw the hordes of Zombies coming and so were forced to retreat into Eternity, to where Janno had shown us to escape. We left a trail for you to follow but when we checked up on that trail we only found Yuan traversing it.}

{Yuan is here?} Peff asked.

{Yes he is} Cheynne answered.

{We were looking for him when we found Sebb} Janno thought.

{We were about to send out a search party} Cheynne thought back.

{That's comforting to know} Sebb thought, {At least you guys haven't forgotten about me.}

{Janno!} Troy thought, {you're back! You're not here to stay are you?}

{No} Janno answered, {I'm just visiting.}

{It's grown dangerous out there during the last few sessions} Troy said.

{We're getting by} Janno thought, {we're here for Yuan.}

{Here I am!} Yuan thought, {Janno, Peff, this is such an exciting place!}

{Don't get too used to it} Peff thought, {we're heading back.}

{Just give me a moment to talk to Sebb.} Yuan thought.

{That'll give us some time to catch up on events.} Troy thought to Janno.   They walked away through Eternity. {Janno? We've confronted an entity traversing through the spectrum claiming to be from another time frame. He also claims that he knows you.}

{That is Father Adam.} Janno exposed, {You should have somewhere in your theories knowledge of him.}

{Janno, you are talking about God.} Troy defined.

{God is just a title of a continuous present actualized being that has existed always even before time began. Adam is a time traveler. He meets the description despite his technology. He qualifies to hold such title however his machine was damaged by the frequencies of the High Command and needs to repair so he's seeking a way to materialize into our time frame to secure the needed particles. Unfortunately there is the High Command causing Father to skip over the frequencies of present time and so he's bouncing uncontrollably into the future, the past, but not the present until a homing beacon has been established. Then he will descend to take us home into Eternity after destroying the High Command.}

{Do you realize that you're suggesting death? No man can enter Eternity alive.} Taylor argued.

{I've spoken to him. I haven't acquired all the schematics but he really is my father genetically.}

{There is so much upon to meditate. I'm going to need time to find answers. We'll continue this conversation.}

{Time is of an essence. I'll swing by at another future.} Janno agreed.

{Sebb, man, am I glad to see you} Yuan thought.

{What's going on Yuan?} Sebb thought.

{Fatima had a baby boy!} Yuan thought.

{She did?!} Sebb thought excitedly.

{A healthy bouncing little Razz!} Yuan thought.

{I'm a father!} Sebb thought, {I'm a father!}

{That's not all} Yuan continued, {Arlos and Arco want to give him the Tub Test.}

{What, the Tub Test?!} Sebb thought, {Why, of course! He's my son. I want him initiated into the ranks of Sentries.}

{But, Sebb} Yuan thought, {that's part of the old ways. We

are no longer serving the System. Everything should be made a new. The baby should be allowed to choose what he wants to be.}

{No. Don't get me wrong. The baby will have a choice} Sebb thought, {The Tub Test is just a way to distinguish survival potential.}

{But, Sebb} Yuan thought, {What if he doesn't make it to the surface. We all would then have killed him.}

{Don't let him drown} Sebb thought, {Just give him seven seconds to reach the surface and if he doesn't make it, pull him out. The worst that could happen is that he won't get to learn the secrets of the Sentry.}

{You make it sound so easy} Yuan thought.

{It is easy} Sebb thought, {I don't want my son to grow without the opportunity to learn what it means to be a Sentry.}

{How about an outlaw?} Yuan thought.

{That's not funny} Sebb thought, {The Code of Honor shared between us demands that my son be given the chance. If he fails, he can just be a classified 3-A}

{If you so wish it, Sebb} Yuan thought, {I just didn't want to go through with it without your approval.}

{You're a pal, Yuan.} Sebb thought.

CHAPTER TWENTY THREE
SECTION FOUR: ETERNITY

{So what do you think of Eternity?} Cheynne asked Peff.

{It's awfully quiet} Peff answered.

{We thought to be at peace in the astral plane} Cheynne thought {but that peace was threatened by the frequencies of the High Command and we were force to retreat here. Janno cordoned off this part of space using eight satellite receptors vibrating at two times the speed of light making existence here drawn into the astral plane, a cube surrounding the planet. The spectrum of colors can take us into any reality within the astral plane, but in Eternity there are no colors. Everything is white here.}

{That's easy to perceive} Peff thought.

{Would you like to see our observation deck?} Cheynne asked.

{Aren't you supposed to be guarding the doorway?} Peff questioned.

{It's Stick Shift's turn} Cheynne said, {He'll be here soon to relieve me.} Just at that moment, Stick Shift appeared to relieve Cheynne.

{What's the sign?} Stick Shift asked.

{The Token of Brotherhood} Cheynne answered.

{And the pass word?}, he inquired.

{Thunder Storm} Cheynne replied.

{Ok} Stick Shift thought, {I'll see you guys later.} Cheynne and Peff walked away through infinity. Stick Shift stayed behind guarding the doorway between the veil and Eternity.

{Here we have our view screens.} Cheynne explained, {One for each pyramid satellite receptor.}

{Those are pretty large view screens} Peff thought.

{They're not only for viewing} Cheynne thought, {they're for transportation also. I should say teleportation.}

{I don't get it} Peff admitted.

{Stand before the second screen} Cheynne thought.

{What's going to happen?} Peff questioned.

{We're going to traverse time and space to observe an event.} Peff stood before the second view screen. Cheynne joined him. The view screen changed its view at one frame per three seconds. {We'll have just a brief moment to jump into the scene shown by the view screen.}, Cheynne thought, {this is how we're observing events past and present, happening in the astral plane and reality.}

{The view screens are portals?} Peff questioned in thought.

{Exactly!} Cheynne thought. {Now hold whatever thoughts you

may have. We're at the right scene. Get ready to jump in.}

{Jump in?} Peff questioned.

{All you have to do is think it} Cheynne thought. The view screen showed a large glass bubble filled with water. In it was a baby infant strapped with a tiny oxygen mask. Tubes and wires came in and out of the baby's small body. Cheynne and Peff stepped through the view screen. In a blinding flash they were transported elsewhere.

{Where are we going?} Peff asked.

{To the High Command's Central Core Chambers} Cheynne thought.

{We've left Eternity, haven't we?} Peff questioned.

{Yes we have} Cheynne answered.

{Shouldn't we have had told somebody we were leaving?} Peff asked.

{Janno is being shown other things at the view screens, as we speak} Cheynne thought. {He left Eternity before we did. Don't worry. We'll be getting back soon enough.}

{I can't hold this form for long} Peff thought.

{Just remain calm} Cheynne thought.

{My pattern is breaking up} Peff thought, {I can't hold it together.}

<Intruder Alert! Intruder Alert!> said the High Command

sensors. <MDV frequency in Astral Plane. Intruder Alert! Activate Astral Sentinel Units to investigate.>

{Damn it! There's no time to demonstrate the need to eliminate the Tub Facilities. We have to get back!} Cheynne said, {The Zombies are coming.}

{I can't hold together!} Peff thought. "I can't hold together!" he said as he awoke inside the tent at the infirmary. Outside the tent, he could hear a small group of people arguing.

CHAPTER TWENTY THREE
SECTION FIVE: INITIATION

"There's no way you're taking this baby for your Tub sport!" Nica said.

"It's not a sport" Arco said, "It's an initiation!"

278

Peff came out of the tent. "Keep it down, people! We have the ill to worry about!" he said, "What's going on?"

These Sentries want to take Fatima's child and dump it into a barrel of water" Nica protested.

"The Tub Test?" Peff asked.

"That's right boss man" Arlos said.

"We can't do that without the parents' approval." Peff said.

"That's the whole problem" Nica said, "These boneheads are trying to brainwash Fatima into thinking that this is a good thing."

"It is a good thing" Arco said.

"Alright, simmer down!" Peff said, "Yuan had contact with Sebb in the astral plane. We'll find out what they spoke about as soon as Yuan comes to. Janno is in the astral plane as well. We need to keep it quiet so that they can have better concentration in their tasks than I did. Until they arrive, we'll leave this matter alone. If we are going to go through with it, every sentry will need to be present. If we are not going to go through with it, it doesn't matter."

"That's not good enough!" Nica protested.

"It'll have to do for now" Peff said.

CHAPTER TWENTY THREE
SECTION SIX: TAYLOR

The Zombies strode forth surrounding the High Command's Central Core Chamber. After having had come aware of the existence of the astral plane, the High Command spared no time in assimilating such an existence to match with its frequency. It guarded itself from any threat whether it emerged from reality or the astral plane.

<Sentinel Unit 89 in function and fully operational> said the Zombie, <No MDV virus detected. Scanning for intrusion>

{I have to escape} Cheynne thought, {It was dangerous to traverse out from Eternity. We should have waited longer.} Cheynne leaped into the void. He traversed across it heading for the veil. Below him he could see a lone and dreary road. Someone was walking across it. He descended to have a closer look.

{Hello there} Cheynne thought.

{Who?} asked the figure.

{My name is Cheynne} he thought, {What's yours?}

{I'm Taylor} thought the figure.

{What are you doing here on this deserted road?} Cheynne asked.

{I do not know.} Taylor thought, {The last thing I remember is I fell asleep. I seem to be lost.}

{Do you believe in thunder?} Cheynne asked.

{I know of a violent storm} Taylor answered.

{You must come with me} Cheynne thought, {It isn't safe for

us to travel through this road for now.}

CHAPTER TWENTY THREE
SECTION SEVEN: DEPARTURE

Inside Eternity: {It is the only way, Janno} thought Troy.

{It sounds dangerous} Janno thought, {But then again anything we may do to bring down the downfall of the High Command could be considered dangerous.}

{Good luck to you, Janno} Troy thought, {May the blessings of the Most High be upon you.}

{Yuan?!} Janno called out, {We're leaving!}   Janno awoke inside the tent at the infirmary. Yuan awakened.   He stepped outside the tent. Outside the tent, argument over Fatima's baby continued.

"I told you to leave the baby alone!" Nica screamed.

"Hold it!" Yuan yelled, "Hold it!"

"Yuan?!" Arlos called, "You're alright!"

"Yes. I'm fine!" Yuan agreed, "I have news directly from Sebb. He wants us to go ahead and give the baby the Tub Test."

"That's crazy!" Nica protested, "You'll kill the child."

"Never under estimate the will to survive!" Arlos said.

"We still need the mother's approval" Peff said.

"Of course I want my baby to grow to be like his father" Fatima said.

"Fatima, you're delirious!" Nica said.

"You shouldn't be up and moving about, Fatima" Vette said.

"I won't let you do it!" Nica said taking hold of the baby.

"Nica?! Let go of my child!" Fatima said.

"You'll kill it!" Nica protested, "I won't let you do it!"

"Everybody freeze!" Janno hollered, "The Tub Test is not needed this day!"

"What?!" Arlos questioned.

"Janno is senior rank!" Arco yelled.

"Agreed!" Peff said, "But we require an explanation."

"Sebb was Sentry Rank One!" Janno said, "That makes the baby Alpha Rank One! He does not need the Tub Test because the Code of Honor gives him all the rights and privileges to learn Sentry matters as a Son of a Sentry Rank One, without the need for the test!"

"Of course!" Peff said, "Something about the Tub Test was not right for this baby."

"We are rebels!" Janno continued, "We serve the system no longer. We cannot follow in the System's paths. We can maintain an order by allowing our Code of Honor to govern over us. And our Code of Honor involves trust and respect.

We trust that the baby can reach the surface. We believe this. There is no need to put it to a trial. He is a Son of a Sentry Rank

One and carries such qualities in his genes. And we respect Sebb's memory and his Rank One status and we will not cast doubt upon his son."

"That makes a lot of sense!" Astian said.

"I'm glad you're back with us, Janno" Orge said.

"Me too!" Yuan agreed.

"All right!" Janno said, "Now that that's cleared, we move up to others matters at hand. The baby needs clothing. I've given up my T-shirt and invite you Sentries to do the same with yours as a gesture of initiation for the baby. It'll be a sign of respect for his birth."

"I agree!" Peff said and he unzipped his jump suit to the waist line and removed his T-shirt. The other sentries did the same.

"Thank-you, Janno!" Nica said.

"That's Ok" Janno said, "Just take it easy and give the baby back to his mother."

"I'm sorry, Fatima" Nica said, "Here's your baby."

"It's Ok, Nica" Fatima said, "I know you were trying to do what you believed to be right."

"I didn't want to see the baby drown." she said.

"He wouldn't have drowned" Fatima said with confidence. She took her baby and hugged it.

"Excuse me" Vette said, "But I think those T-shirts stink. They need to be washed."

"Why don't we place them in the barrel?" Arco said.

"Good idea!" Astian said, "I saw some yucca plants not too far from here. We can use them as soap."

"I'll do the washing" Nica volunteered.

"I'll give you a hand" Vette said.

"Peff?" Janno said, "I'm sorry I had to take command."

"Oh don't worry about that" Peff said, "You're the man. The Code of Honor shared between us defines that."

"What's the command structure around here?" Janno asked.

"Luna is in charge" Peff said, "We have three fighting units. I head Unit Alpha One. Alpha One is composed of Sentries. Unit Alpha Two is headed by Ace and is composed of non-sentry Seniors. Unit Alpha Three is headed by Jeppe and his team is composed of all Juniors. Team Alpha One is yours to lead."

"I don't think that would be appropriate" Janno said.

"Oh? Why not?" Peff asked.

"I've just gotten here" Janno answered, "I don't think it is right to suddenly usurp command."

"If you say so, Janno" Peff said, "But any time you want to lead us, just say the word." Just then Rex and the Lost Boys came along.

"We've finished with our assessment of Taylor" Rex said. "He mentioned someone named Cheynne that he dreamt about."

"Janno is more equipped to converse with Taylor. I suspect your friend will soon metamorphose."

"Is there anything we can do to help out?" Lyman asked.

"Night is falling on us again" Peff said, "We have the perimeter secured. We'll have a meeting tomorrow at zero nine hundred hours. That's all. We can bed down for the night."

CHAPTER TWENTY FOUR

SECTION ONE: PERIMETER SCOUTS

The next morning, Janno and the Lost Boys walked up to the

perimeters of sector Chi 7, quadrant 4. <Halt! Who goes there?!> Lisa asked.

"It's me, Janno!" he responded.

<State your purpose!> Lisa demanded.

"To scout the crash site" Janno said.

<That could be dangerous> Lisa said. <I'll have to inform the Unit Commander. Omega Two to Alpha One, Omega Two to Alpha One, Come in Alpha One; Over!>

<This is unit Alpha One, Over!> Jeppe said.

<Alpha One, we have an intruder at the perimeter. Over!> Lisa said.

<Have you identified him? Over!> Jeppe asked.

<He claims to be Janno. Over!> Lisa answered.

<In what direction did he come from? Over> Jeppe asked.

<He came from the direction of the campsite. Over!> Lisa replied.

<That's not an intruder, Lisa. Over!> Jeppe said.

<He wants to scout the crash site. Over!> Lisa said.

<I'll be right there. Over!> Jeppe said.

<Roger that: Alpha One. This is Omega Two, out!> Lisa said, <He's on his way over here, Janno.>

"Thank you, Lisa" Janno said.

"Political delay" Lyman remarked.

"Easy, Lyman" Rex ordered, "The Razzs are just doing their job."

"Are you late for an appointment?" Gormely asked Lyman.

"I'm just feeling queasy over Taylor's metamorphose." he responded.

"I know what you mean" Allen said, "I can't believe that our theories have become law."

"I'm sure he will be safe and well in the astral plane" Janno said.

"I still gotta get used to this." Ruffer said.

"Why do you want to scout the crash site, Janno?" Rex asked.

"I thought maybe we could use the armor the fallen Sentinels have." Janno answered.

"You want to cannibalize the Sentinels?" Lyman asked.

"I want to locate the frequency their using to operate on." Janno answered.

"How is this going to help us?" Ruffer asked.

"We can duplicate the frequency and communicate with the High Command" Janno replied.

"Communication with the High Command?" Gormely questioned.

"We can easily infiltrate the system that way" Rex responded.

"That makes sense" Allen said.

<Janno?!> Jeppe called out.

"Jeppe?" Janno answered, "How are you?" Jeppe removed his helmet.

"I'm fine. What brings you out here? You're not my relief, are you?"

"We want to go out to the crash site" Lyman said.

"No problem" Jeppe said, "I'll have you escorted. There could be trouble."

"I need you to come along, Jeppe" Janno said.

"I'll be with you in a moment" Jeppe said, "Just let me give my team proper commands." Jeppe donned his helmet on. <Alpha One to all Units. Team Alpha One and Two: you're coming with me. Omega One and Two: you're staying behind. This is Alpha One, out!>

<Ok, gentlemen> Jeppe said, <We can move out now>

"He's good at giving orders, isn't he?" Ruffer said.

"At ease" Rex commanded, "It's their show." Jeppe moved out ahead in the direction of the crash site. Behind him were Janno and the Lost Boys. Team Alpha Two was to the right of them and Team Alpha Three was to the left. They moved out in formation through the rugged sand terrain. The wind blew sand in their faces.

<Birds!> Angie pointed out through her helmet.

<Where?> Vikki asked, <I don't see any>

<Those aren't just birds!> Jeppe said, <They're buzzards>

"They're probably feeding off the dead Sentinels!" Lyman said.

"We had better get there soon." Rex said. They arrived at the site. Janno went directly to the Gasto Unit. "We're going to have to bury them." Janno said.

"They're half buried already!" Taylor said.

"Then we'll need to uncover them." Allen said.

"Jeppe, I need you with me" Janno said. He uncovered the

Gasto Unit's helmet and removed it. "There's a blinking light on this one."

<It's probably a location monitor> Jeppe said.

"Are you sure?" Janno asked.

"More Sentinels could be coming." Allen said.

<I'm not so sure of that> Jeppe said, <but just in case, Alpha Two and Alpha Three: dig yourselves a position. Alpha Two: you have the right flank. Alpha Three: you have the left> Jeppe removed his helmet. "It's some kind of tracking system." Jeppe said referring to the blinking light on the Gasto Unit's helmet.

"Are you sure, Jeppe?" Janno asked.

"We'll check the other Sentinels to see if they have the same light on their helmets." Rex said.

"I think I can hook it up to my armor" Jeppe said, "I have a computer screen inside my chest plate." Jeppe took the Gasto Unit helmet and plugged a cord into a slot by the blinking light. He then reconnected a few cords in his armor. Then:

<Unit Alpha 3 Mark 215, this is Unit Sigma 5 Digit One: come in Digit Six!>

"It's a communication channel!" Jeppe said.

"Can it hear us?" Janno asked.

"No. Not unless I communicate back with it." Jeppe said.

"What does it want?" Janno asked.

"It wants the Digit Six to acknowledge." Jeppe said.

"Send a message!" Janno said, "Use the same frequency."

"What do you want I should say?" Jeppe asked.

"Acknowledge!" Janno said. Jeppe donned his helmet on.

<This is Unit Alpha 3 Mark 215; come in Digit One, over!> Jeppe said reading the serial number within the Gasto Unit's helmet.

<Digit Six, This is Digit One requesting activity report> said the

Digit One. Jeppe took his helmet off.

"It wants an activity report." he told Janno. Jeppe put his helmet on.

"Repeat this, Jeppe" Janno said, "Digit Six Activity Report is a follows; MDV carriers located. Carriers deleted. Prisoners in custody: Prisoners on standby for assimilation and reassignment: Will rendezvous at Unit Sigma 5, E.T.A.: eight sessions, over!"

Jeppe repeated Janno's words. <Copy that, Digit Six, Unit Sigma 5 Digit One, out!> said the Digit One. Jeppe took his helmet off.

"They bought it, Janno", Jeppe said.

"Good! We have to move fast now" Janno said, "We don't have much time. I'll have to let the Lost Boys know what has been done."

"I'll strip the Sentinel from his armor." Jeppe said.

"How did it go?" Ruffer asked.

"We've managed to communicate with Unit Sigma 5" Janno said.

"What's the plan?" Lyman asked.

"We're infiltrating Sigma 5 as prisoners and Sentinels" Janno said.

"We can then attain access to the Central Core Chambers." Rex said.

"And deactivate the Tub facilities." Allen said.

"Don't forget the assimilation monitor." Gormely added.

"How much time do we have?" Rex asked.

"I gave an ETA of eight sessions." Janno said.

"That's more than enough time" Ruffer said.

"We'll have time to bury these Sentinels." Rex said.

"They're lighter without their armor" Janno said, "Let's get their armor and laser guns off, and head back to camp with the defunct bodies." Janno and the Lost Boys recovered the fallen armor while Jeppe and his team maintained the position secured.

CHAPTER TWENTY FOUR
SECTION TWO: PERIMETER CHECK

At the perimeter: <Halt! Who goes there?!> Lisa said.

<This is Team Leader Alpha One and the Lost Boys> Jeppe replied.

<State your purpose?!> Lisa asked.

<To gain access to the campsite> Jeppe responded.

<How do I know you're not a Sentinel?> Lisa demanded.

<Lisa? Sentinels wouldn't function underneath the frequency shield> Jeppe said.

<Oh, yeah! That's right!> Lisa said, <I forgot. Ok you can pass>

"You've trained them well, Jeppe." Lyman said.

<I try> Jeppe said, <Attention Team Alpha Three, this is Alpha One to all units. Pick up your gear, help carry the dead, and let's get back to camp. We have a meeting at zero nine hundred hours. Alpha One, out!>

"What's this meeting all about?" Rex asked.

<It's where we let each other know what's going on> Jeppe responded.

CHAPTER TWENTY FOUR
SECTION THREE: WAR COUNCIL

Later at the campsite: "Thunder Storm Warriors?! Unite!"

Luna had called out. Everyone from seniors to juniors rallied around her. "Peff?!" she questioned, "Report status!"

"Armor removed from the Sentinels is now in Team X's use" Peff answered.

"Team X?" Luna asked.

"Janno and the Lost Boys are now functioning as Team X" Peff replied, "Strategy plan to invade Sigma 5 is complete. We will infiltrate as Sentinels and prisoners. Radio frequencies have been adapted for High Command Frequency Code ^ ^ #* use. Second frequency is for Thunder Storm use."

"Satisfactory" Luna answered. "Medical?"

"We don't have any supplies" Nica answered, "We're relying on the frequent metamorphosis periods from Peff to alleviate any maladies as well as hunger. Janno and Yuan have matured. Fatima and her baby are well. Taylor is supposed to metamorphose but hasn't done so yet."

"No problem" Luna answered, "We'll just have to raid a nutrient capsule and bring it back if we get the chance. Alright, everybody: suit up! We'll be moving out in point two sessions. Thunder Storm?! In effect!!"

"Hold it!" Rex said.

"Oh?" Luna mumbled.

"What seems to be the problem, Rex?" Peff asked.

"There's too many people going" Rex said.

"Are we going all out?" Lyman asked, "Some of you may not return."

"We are all aware of the danger," Luna said, "but we have our faith and we have our convictions."

"My point is that a small group of fighters can maneuver a lot better and a lot faster than a whole mass."

"We would be detected easily if too many people go." Ruffer said.

"If we're going to go all out, we might as well attack the High Command Central Core Chambers and forget about Sigma 5." Allen said.

"You do not want us to go with you?" Luna asked.

"You would serve a better purpose elsewhere" Rex replied.

"Peff?!" Luna cried, "I want to review the battle plan, now."

"Team X will be escorted by Team Alpha One as prisoners" Peff said, "Upon entering Unit Sigma 5 both teams will split up; team Alpha One will head for the Central Core Chamber while Team X will capture the Assimilation Annex for monitor neutralization."

"What about Team Alpha Two and Three?" Luna asked.

"They would be on standby; lying in wait outside the perimeters of unit Sigma 5." Janno answered.

"At what point would they be used?" Luna questioned.

"They wouldn't be used at all." Ruffer answered.

"There's a probability that they may hinder our escape, should we need to abort the mission." Lyman said.

"We held our ground when you first arrived crashing the transport shuttle at our perimeters" Luna said, "We will hold our ground at the perimeter of Sigma 5."

"All units suit up!" Peff called out.

"Peff?!" Luna cried out, "We need medical to stay behind with Fatima and a small skeleton crew at the perimeter."

"Roger that: Luna!" Peff said, "Ace, give me Omega Two to stay behind with Fatima."

"You've got it!" Ace said.

"Jeppe, I need Omega One and Two to stay behind at the perimeter." Peff called out.

"In effect!" Jeppe called back. And with everything said and done Thunder Storm mobilized itself for a long march across the desert terrain or so Rex thought. They marched in formation to the perimeters of sector Chi 7, quadrant 4. <Team Three Alpha One to Team Three Omega One and Two!> Jeppe said through his helmet, <Luani, Litra, Lisa, and Sajie: take your positions. You have perimeter duty until we get back: any questions?>

<This is Omega One, loud and clear!> Luani and Litra said.

<This is Omega Two, roger that Alpha One!> said Lisa and Sajie.

The rest of the team kept marching to the crash site. <Team Leader Alpha One to all Units, radio check, over!> Peff said.

<This is Team Leader X, I read you loud and clear!> said Rex.

<This is Team X Alpha Two, we read you!> said Allen and Ruffer.

<Team X Alpha Three: loud and clear!> said Lyman and Gormely.

<Alpha One Alpha Two: loud and clear!> said Astian and Arco.

<Alpha One Alpha Three: loud and clear!> said Orge and Yuan.

<Team Leader Alpha Two Alpha One, roger that!> reported Ace.

<Team Alpha Two Alpha Two, we copy!> said Queen and Alaetra.

<Alpha Two Alpha Three, we hear you!> said Chic and Weena.

<Alpha Two Omega One: roger!> said Nette and Betty.

<Team Leader Alpha Three Alpha One, I copy, over!> reported Jeppe.

<Alpha Three Alpha Two, roger!> said Vikki and Angie.

<Alpha Three Alpha Three, we copy!> said Deena and Tina.

<Alpha Three Omega One and Two are at the rear> Jeppe said.

<Radio check confirmed!> said Peff, <Attention Team X and Alpha One, dig yourselves a position to the left of the crash site. Team Alpha Two and Three, you guys got the right side> They moved on command as if rehearsed a thousand times. Team One had done this before. They were going to recapture a Refuse Transport Shuttle.

<Alright Teams!> Peff called out, <When I set off this frequency jamming device the shuttle will come to a complete halt. Team Alpha One Alpha Two will then switch on the transmitter device and attach it to the forepart of the

truck. Alpha One Alpha Two will then hop aboard the shuttle. Are there any questions?> There were none. <Good! All we do now is sit tight and wait> But then Peff called out, <Here it comes! On my mark...now!>

ℭHAPTER TWENTY FIVE

SECTION ONE: BLUE GEMINI

"ℬlue Gemini to Mission Control, come in Mission Control!' said the Voice.

"Nica!" Vette called out, "Tell Luna that thing is talking!" Luna hearing Vette call out came running.

"What thing?" She asked, "What thing?" She propped herself up before the controls, "Hello?

Hello? This is Luna. Hello?" She clicked the controls.

"Mission Control, what seems to be the problem, over?"

"Mission Control?" Luna asked, "Who's mission control?"

"Stand by please…"

{Father, are you sure we can trust Janno to do what we set him out to do?} Troy asked.

{He won't let us down. He's done a lot. Even if existence weren't in trouble he would still come to our aid.}, answered the Voice.

{I just hope it were he at the communication channel} said Troy, {We'll try again}. "Thunder Storm?" Troy asked.

"Yes, yes!" Luna said with excitement, "This is Thunder Storm! This is Thunder Storm!"

"Thunder Storm you're coordinates are now Mission Control, is that understood?" Troy directed.

"Thunder Storm, mission control, yes, I receive, uh, copy over."

"Mission Control?" inquired the Voice, "Is the radar homing device built?"

"Yes, the frequency shield, the jamming device, and platform? Yes, yes, we have them built!"

"Stand by Mission Control"

{Frequency shield platform, Troy?}, the Voice asked.

{You should have heard all the other names used throughout the generations. I mean they've called it the Land Mine, The Air Strip, the Buttocks, the-}

{I get the point} said the Voice, "Mission Control this is Blue Gemini."

"This is Mission Control, over" Luna said.

"Mission Control, switch nuclear laser sights, On!" said the Voice.

"Nuclear sights? What are nuclear sights?" Luna asked {Oh Jeppe, I should have had been paying more attention instead of trying to kiss you!} "Nica!"

"Mission Control, what is your name young lady?" asked the Voice

"I am Luna" She answered.

"Luna, this is Blue Gemini, pay close attention, honey" said the Voice.

"Nica?" Luna whispered, "send for Lisa and Sajie"

CHAPTER TWENTY FIVE
SECTION TWO: STRATEGIC REVIEW

Meanwhile inside a Refuse Transport Shuttle: "We're a few clicks from the perimeters to Sigma 5" Peff said, "Let's go over the plan one last time."

"I am Rex, team leader to be hexed at the Central Core Chambers I am to apply my specs. Janno is my partner I will not fear. He will rapport. He will commandeer." said Rex.

"I am Janno, once Ojahn One, I am to make sure Rex gets the job done." Janno spoke.

"To the Assimilation Monitor is where we go. We make the major hook up and then we blow." said Taylor spoke for Team X.

"To the Ice Tub containment units we will ride and execute Sentinel anti-genocide." announced the ex-Warrior Unit.

"We dig a position, we dig it outside. If you're not out in a session then we come inside" said Teams Alpha Two and Three.

"I'm pretty nervous" Ruffer said, "But if blowing up the Assimilation Monitors means I get my soul back then it's worth it."

"We all want a piece of that machine." Gormely added.

"Air" Arco said removing his helmet, "I need air. I'm hyperventilating."

"We're too close to turn back now" Orge said.

"That's not the half of it" Astian said, "How many of us are in here?"

"It does seem somewhat crowded" Arlos said.

"Rex is Team X leader; that's one." Peff said, "Allen, Ruffer, Taylor, Lyman, and Gormely are the rest of team X; that's another four."

"I'm independent but attached to team X." Janno said, "That makes me six."

"I'm seven." Peff added, "Team Alpha One: Two and Three make it twelve."

"I'm thirteen." said Ace, "Team Alpha Two: One, Two, and Three make it nineteen."

"That leaves me at twenty." said Jeppe, "Team Alpha Three: Two and Three end it at twenty five."

"Man, it smells like feet and socks it here" Arco said placing his helmet back on.

"We're at the perimeter!" Peff announced, "Everybody standby." The Truck came to a slow down. "All Teams jump out when the door is opened!"

"Don't goof it up this time, Gormely!" Rex said.

"You can count on me, Chief!" Gormely operated the gears and the truck came to a halt. The doors then slid open.

"Out!" Peff commanded, "Everybody out!" All twenty five Thunder Storm personnel jumped out. Team Alpha Two and Three took their position near the perimeters of Sigma 5 and began digging their fox holes. Rex and Janno made their move to the Central Core Chambers. Allen, Ruffer, Lyman and Gormely made their move to the Assimilation Monitors while Peff, Astian, Arlos, Arco, Orge, and Yuan made their way to the Ice Tub Facilities

CHAPTER TWENTY FIVE
SECTION THREE: BAIT

"Honey, relax, you can do this" said the Voice.

"I'm scared, Sir, I'm afraid I might make a mistake" Luna said.

"Don't think that way" said the Voice, "Just concentrate on my voice. I'll guide you through."

"If you say so, Sir" Luna said nervously.

"Describe to me the lay outs of the control monitors before you" said the Voice, "Which is the largest switch or lever?"

"There's a big red button, but that activates the frequency shielding." Luna said.

"Let's try that." said the Voice, "Ignite!"

"Ig-what?" Luna inquired.

"Turn it on, honey" said the Voice.

"Oh, I feel like an amateur" Luna said.

"You're doing fine, honey" said the Voice, "We just have a problem with terminology. Don't worry. We'll get through."

{That appears to have lighted the space buoys} Troy thought.

{She's doing fine} thought the Voice, {Without her help we won't be able to navigate the ship home.}

{This is all so cool} Sebb thought.

{Isn't it though} Cheynne thought, {they'll be so surprised to see all of us. Imagine what they might think when they realize we have Father with us.}

{And all this time} Stick Shift added, {I was curious to know what happens after we die? We just go to another dimension, a different place in space. Sweet!}

{We're lucky Father came by when he did} Cheynne commented.

{It's frightening to think what might have happen if we were left behind} Stick Shift thought {The High Command exists solely to engulf whatever frequency it may encounter. If a computer program to alphabetize names were in progress, and the High Command came across it, then the High Command would swallow that program and increase in power and gaining ability to alphabetize names. Now imagine gaining all knowledge in the astral plane which is limitless.}

{The High Command is trying to take over Father's existence} Cheynne added, {What gall! Not that Father is a computer program but it's the same, the Alpha waves and thought patterns exist in the same realm. If the High Command wins, our freedom is forfeit.}

{This is going to be a big fight.} Stick Shift thought.

{It's no fight at all.} Troy thought {we simply lure the High Command to an irresistible source of infinite power and when we lure it there, we shut it down.}

{But where are we going to get a source of unlimited power?} Sebb thought.

{No, not Father.} Cheynne whispered.

"That's it! You're doing great" Father said, "Now pull the lever down and the automatic navigation systems should maneuver us in through the rest of space until we reach earth's orbit."

"Thank you Daddy" Luna said, "I mean Father, for believing in me!"

"I love you too, sweetheart" Father said. Luna had launched a laser beneath Blue Gemini. The laser took hold of the nucleus of an atom and spun it around at 180,000 rotations per second. This caused a portal to open beneath the Time Capsule Blue Gemini and guided into the atmosphere as a magnetic tractor beam.

CHAPTER TWENTY FIVE
SECTION FOUR: ARRESTED

"There doesn't seem to be anyone out here" Janno said, "Do you think it might be a trap?"

"What we know about the Outer System is that it functions perfectly," Rex said suited up in Sentinel gear holding Janno as his prisoner, "As long as we do not pose a danger to any of the High Commands systems, we're in no threat."

"All this silence is very unnerving" Janno admitted.

"What were Gasto's call signs?" Rex asked

"Alpha 3 Mark 215" Janno answered.

<This is Sentinel Unit Alpha 3 Mark 215 to Unit Sigma 5 Central Core Chamber Digit One> Rex said through the Sentinel Helmet.

CHAPTER TWENTY FIVE
SECTION FIVE: WHICH WAY TO GO?

<All right, fellows> Allen said suited up in Sentinel armor and leading his team, <Let's veer through this passage way and we should be where we need to be to keep up with our time slot>

"No." Ruffer said, as a prisoner, "Not that way. Over here."

"Are you sure?" Gormely questioned, as the second prisoner.

<System lay outs are all the same> Lyman said in Sentinel armor, <If the Assimilation Monitors

are where Ruffer thinks they are then we should have no problem finding them here>

"I have a strange gut feeling we should go with Ruffer." Gormely said.

<But the maps> Allen protested.

<We're wasting time arguing> Lyman said

"With the way we're going" Gormely said, "I'm surprised we haven't been caught yet."

<Make a decision> Lyman requested. Allen crumbled up the maps.

<We'll go with Ruffer> he said. Ruffer led the way. The rest followed.

CHAPTER TWENTY FIVE
SECTION SIX: THE ICE TUBS

Arco and Orge, in Sentinel armor held Astian, Arlos, and Yuan in check at the Ice Tube facilities.

"Can you believe it all?" Yuan asked.

<How come you're not causing any system malfunctions?> Arco asked him.

"I really don't know how it works." Yuan confessed.

"No one knows how it works." Taylor agreed, "Any one of us could change right about now."

<We had better get to do what we came here to do> Orge said.

"This is all so weird" Arlos commented, "We came from facilities similar to these. It was because of our ability to survive such ordeals that we banded together through a code of honor, a code of respect, a code for life"

"You said it yourself, Arlos." Astian said, "A code for life. The mutation has caused problems with the Tub Facilities. The Razzies are being born deformed with no possible chance for surviving the test. It's an inhuman thing the High Command does to submerge newborns into ice water without hope for survival."

<Bbrrrr!> Arco remarked, <That brings back cold memories>

"According to Lyman a major percentage was failing to survive" Yuan said.

<That's why we're here> Orge said <to destroy these facilities>

"I'll log on to the computers manually and override any monitoring procedures." Yuan said.

<I'll plug into the communication network and keep an ear open> Orge said.

<I'll stand by for incoming Sentinels>" Arco said.

"That leaves Arlos and me, to rewire this entire sight to blow itself up from a power surge at main power source." Astian said.

"All we have to do is remove the power surge fuse cable" Arlos said. And the boys quietly went about their business.

"I know it was discussed that we save these babies. But it was also recognized that it would be a lesser of two evils to abort their lives than to allow them to live with deformities only to encumber a weight of responsibilities on their care takers if we had any to begin with. It hurts me to do what we have to do" Yuan said, "But these children will grow to reach Maturity upon the Return or Restoration of all things and in a perfect condition."

CHAPTER TWENTY FIVE
SECTION SEVEN:PRISONER TRANSFER

<This is Sigma 5 Digit One, come in Alpha 3, over>

<Sigma 5 Digit One, this is Alpha 3 Mark 215: have in custody element Janno Ojahn One: Element: in standby for Initialization Sequence: Request Comm Link

with Central Core Chambers and Unit Delta 6 Digit One Assimilation Monitor for reanimation>

<Standby Alpha 3: Comm link initiated> The High Command desired knowledge. Janno's play book stolen by Gasto and found in his possession had reached the awareness of the High Command earlier when Janno and Gasto were first delivered to Sigma 5. The High Command had analyzed the logic written therein. The High Command wanted to assimilate it for itself. Janno's abilities were wanted. The High Command believed it had assimilated Janno earlier at the Assimilation Monitors of Sigma 5. But now it wanted to see how such believed assimilated abilities worked on the Squabble floor for Sentinel adaptation.

<Transfer Code C Element to Central Core Chambers: Element

is to engage in Ultimate Squabble against the High Command itself. Transmitting HC Priority Code #^%. Sigma 5 Digit One out>

"What's going on?" Janno asked.

<The High Command has challenged you to a game of Squabble> Rex announced, <I'm to take you the Central Core Chambers>

"We better inform the others" Janno said.

<Are you serious?> Rex questioned, <Don't you think we should abort our mission than take a chance playing Squabble against a machine. You'll be killed>

"I'm only the bait." Janno clarified.

CHAPTER TWENTY FIVE
SECTION EIGHT: FATHER IS COMING

"What is it?" Lisa asked

"Oh, Lisa" Luna said, "I'm Ok. I wanted a communication relay to Jeppe. Are the communicators still at the perimeters?"

"Everything is in working condition" Sajie interrupted, "We left Luani and Litra securing the perimeter. If there's nothing to do here, we need to head back."

"I need to send a message to Jeppe." Luna said.

"What would you have us say to him?" Lisa asked.

"I really don't know how to explain what has just happened." Luna said, "Tell him that the frequency shield platform has been activated and a target has been locked on to and will enter the atmosphere shortly. He needs to be here to guide the sensors."

"I think we've better write that down." Sajie said.

"Just tell him I need him." Luna said, "It's an emergency."

"Roger that!" Lisa said, "Let's go Sajie." And the two girls left for the camp's perimeters.

"Luna, is everything alright?" Joan asked.

"I'm sensing an anxiety, I think." She said.

"Would you like to talk about it?" Joan asked.

"It's that voice, the one in the polarity shield" she answered, "I've never heard anything like it before, so calm, so tranquil, so much peace."

"He is coming, isn't he" Joan asked.

"Yes" Luna answered, "I just hope we are all ready to receive him and he us."

"The theories were true, Luna, they were true!" Nica exclaimed. They hugged each other as Vette and Fatima came out of the tent with the baby.

"Father is coming for us" Luna said with a tear in her eye.

"Oh Luna" Fatima pleaded, "Tell us about him"

"I will" Luna said wiping her tears, "The legend said: Let your light so shine forth, that he may see your good works, and in so you will glorify your Father which is in heaven. That is what Jeppe and I have been working on, the light to shine forth which is actually what Jeppe called a radar homing unit. It sends the light out into space for Father to see that we are ready for him. Letting your light shine also means to set a righteous example for others to follow.

I have always believed in the existence of Father. He lives in heaven. Likewise you too must believe in Father and believe that he is and that he created all things both in heaven and in earth. Believe that he has all wisdom, and all power, both in heaven and in earth. It is this wisdom and this power that the High Command wishes to strip him of. It is this wisdom and this power that he wants to bestow upon us who are his children.

Father is perfect. We are his children. It is written in olden records, "The Spirit itself bears witness with our spirit, that we are the children of the Father. We were in the beginning with the Father; that which is spirit even the Spirit of truth. We are eternal having a portion of his spirit.

"So we can be like Father?" Vette asked.

"Yes" Luna agreed

"Why were we separated from him?" Nica asked.

"There is only so much we can accomplish in one place before we have to move on." Luna answered, "There must be room for change, for progress and so we are sent to gain knowledge. Whosoever shall keep Father's regulations receives truth and understanding, until one understands all things. I say these things that you may understand and know Father, and in due time receive his presence. Anyone who rejects the light as the High Command has done is under condemnation."

"Thunder Storm is important isn't it?" Fatima asked.

"It's strange," Vette admitted, "If we would have rejected fulfilling our responsibilities to Thunder Storm, we would not be where we are now."

"Shouldn't the others be alerted?" Nica admitted.

"I've sent a message with the juniors" Luna said, "They should be relaying it by now."

CHAPTER TWENTY FIVE
SECTION NINE: COME IN, JEPPE

"They're taking too long" Ace said anxiously.

"It's not time yet" Jeppe admitted, "There's a quarter session remaining. We have to stand down until time permits us to act."

"It's very hot out here" Queen complained.

"I'm getting thirsty" Betty admitted.

<Alpha Omega Two to Team Leader Three, come in Jeppe, over!>

<This is Team Leader Three, over>

<Jeppe, this is Lisa> she said, <Luna says she needs you back at the polarity platform ASAP.>

<Stand by Omega Two> Jeppe said, <Team Leader Three to Team Leader One, over>

<Peff here, what's going on?> he asked

<This is Team Leader Three> Jeppe acknowledged, <I'm required back at base>

<Standfast, Team Three> Peff said <We're all finished here. Standby for rendezvous>

<Team Leader Three to Omega Two> Jeppe said, <I'll be delayed at least one more session, over>

<I'll relay your message to Luna> Lisa said, <Omega Two, out!>

CHAPTER TWENTY FIVE
SECTION TEN: MISSION ABORT

"How are we going to destroy this thing?" Ruffer asked overlooking the padded assimilation counter.

"We're not going to destroy it" Allen corrected with his helmet off, "We're going to use it. Hop on"

"I'm not hopping on nothing." Ruffer refused.

"I'll do it" Gormely said.

"You don't have to sacrifice yourself for me, Gormely." Ruffer said.

"I'm not doing this for you" Gormely clarified, "I was assimilated once and I want my memories back."

"It's all set" Lyman said, "Rex has linked up to the Central Core Chambers"

"Now, then" Gormely demanded. Allen took control of the monitor and loaded Gormely's identification codes into the monitor and restored Gormely to health.

"How do you feel?" Allen asked. There was no answer but action as Ruffer hopped onto the monitor.

"Punch in my codes before the link is severed!" Ruffer ordered. And in a few moments:

"I feel no different" Gormely confessed.

"Maybe it will take some time" Ruffer said, "Let's blow this place and meet up with the rest of the teams outside."

<Standby, I have a message coming in> Lyman said, <Roger that> "We're required to abort the mission."

"What?" Allen demanded.

"Let's just get out of here before we get caught." Gormely suggested.

"I'm with G." Ruffer agreed. And with that the boys left the Assimilation Monitors alone.

CHAPTER TWENTY FIVE
SECTION ELEVEN: NEW BATTLE PLAN

The three teams reunited and then proceeded to confiscate another refuse transport shuttle and all headed back to base camp. They discussed and debriefed each other on what had happened during their attempt to destroy Sigma 5.

"I don't know how important this may be." Lyman said, "But according to the Birth Records we had confiscated before we met you all, we are all related."

"What do you mean?" Orge questioned.

"We share common genes" Lyman answered, "It's strange though, it's as if those genes had remained dormant in the gene pool of the High Command and appeared not too long ago when we were all conceived."

"So we're all brothers and sisters?" Arco asked.

"No" Lyman answered, "We descend from two different alpha sources or ancestors, primarily. Joseph Adam Lezama, father to Thunder Storm and Abraham Medina Duran, father to the Lost Boys. Their genes somehow managed to enter into the gene pool of the O.G.A.H.N. system and underwent a bottleneck effect that produced us. Some of us are distant cousins, thrice removed, but kin nevertheless." That caught Janno's attention as he looked at Jeena.

"Are we allowed to reproduce?" She asked feeling her face swell red.

351

"I think we are Ok" Lyman said, "For those of you that are transmuting or reaching maturity as you call it, the new genes will provide a variety of gametes to the gene pool."

"What caused this mutation in the first place?" Queen asked.

"It was the High Command's vibration frequencies that altered our chemical make up a little at a time as it vibrated at a radiated level dangerous for existence. At the turn of the twenty first century mankind was living in a highly but complex advanced technological society. Personal communicators, computers, and hand held devices used exposed the brain and body to radiation. Human vision pixilated. These dangers were covered up in the desire to 'make a buck' as they called it then."

"Make a buck?" Vikki asked.

"They had a system of tokens given for good behavior" Jeena answered, "They then used these tokens for trade."

"They were a greedy people" Janno added with disgust, "But it doesn't seem right that we should have to suffer for their mistakes."

"Heads up every one" Peff announced, "We're nearing the crash site."

"Peff?" Arco questioned, "Shouldn't we confiscate the SPC instead of always hi-jacking a refuse truck?"

"That's not such a bad idea" Orge agreed.

"Both of you: get it." Peff ordered, "We'll meet you back at base camp."

"Roger!" Arco said donning on his helmet and jumping out of the truck. Orge followed him. <This is all so overwhelming. Janno has been challenged by the System itself to a game of Squabble. Can you believe it?>

<I believe you want in on the action> Orge said.

<Of course I do> Arco confessed, <Don't you?>

<I admit that I was conditioned for Squabble> Orge confessed, <Playing a game wouldn't be bad at all but we're in a higher plane now. We shouldn't even be thinking about it. That's like placing our lives in the hands of the High Command again. We

might just as well never have escaped>

<Look Orge> Arco explained, <Janno accepted that challenge, perhaps not directly but he did. I'm not going to let him go at it alone>

<He will need a team won't he?> Orge understood.

<Now you're getting it!> Arco said, <With this SPC, we're going to enter the System in style!>

$\mathscr{C}$HAPTER TWENTY SIX

SECTION ONE: THE FINAL SQUABBLE

"$\mathscr{I}$still don't understand why you?" Jeena asked him angrily, "We're together perhaps for the only time in our lives and you want to go and play that stupid game, and with the High Command!"

"Jeena?" Janno said, "You're being irrational, you don't understand."

"Don't you understand?" she said, "I love you!"

"I know you do, honey" Janno confessed, "But I have to do this. If I can do this, we'll be together forever." They hugged each other for comfort.

"Janno, we need to debrief again." Peff said.

CHAPTER TWENTY SIX: SECTION TWO
BATTLE PREPARATIONS

"Only one of us can accompany Janno back to the Central Core Chambers" Rex began, "to turn him into the custody of the Digit One who will prep him for the game. Janno will then choose team players from the Core Campus' Squabble Teams."

"But I thought we were going to back him?" Arco protested.

"That's what the plan is" Rex announced, "But we'll have to find a way inside the Campus for Janno to pick us out."

"There's a passage way built onto the game floor" Jeppe announced pointing at a spot on the make shift map, "Gasto had his companion build it as part of chore assignments. I believe all Campuses have it installed at one point or another otherwise it could not have been approved as a chore assignment."

"We will infiltrate as Sentinels" Arco suggested, "We'll enter the gym and pose as players in time for Janno to pick us out."

"It'll have to do" Janno said.

"All right everyone who's going to suit up, suit up" Rex said, "We have to be at the Central Core Chambers in a quarter sessions."

CHAPTER TWENTY SIX
SECTION THREE: GOOD TIDINGS

"Jeppe!" Luna exclaimed, "He's coming!"

"Who's coming?" Jeppe questioned.

"Father is coming!" she announced.

"How do you know?" Jeppe asked.

"I spoke with him" she answered.

"Is there any way to get him back on channel?" Jeppe asked.

"We're to maintain radio silence until they reach orbit." Luna responded.

"I guess then my place is here next to you." Jeppe said. He sat next to her and she placed a hand in his lap.

"You look rugged." she said.

"A lot has happened" he answered her. They remained quiet starring at the controls to the device they had built, waiting for Father to contact them.

CHAPTER TWENTY SIX .
SECTION FOUR: BACK IN THE SYSTEM

Much later at the perimeters of the Central Core Chambers: "Every one stand by" Rex spoke, "We're going to be identified"

<SPC carrier, identify> said the Central Core Chambers.

<Central Core Chambers, this is SPC Carrier Alpha 3 Mark 215: Element Code C: Janno Ojahn One in custody for transfer to Core Campus, over!>

<215 access Central Core Chambers code #^% confirmed>

"We're in" Rex announced, "Once I station the carrier, I'll escort Janno to the Central Core Chambers. The rest of you wait until its safe, and then sneak out into the locker room."

CHAPTER TWENTY SIX
SECTION FIVE: INTERROGATION

<Let the subject come forth> announced the High Command. Rex, in Sentinel armor led Janno into the High Command's Central Core Chambers. <Subject Identify!> requested the High Command.

"I am Janno Ojahn One" he responded.

<Justify> ordered the High Command.

"I have no justification" Janno responded, "I just am."

<You are an MDV carrier and must be terminated> said the High Command.

361

"I offer a better solution" Janno proposed.

<Awaiting proposal> said the High Command.

"I offer MDV frequencies for assimilation." Janno said.

<To what purpose?> asked the High Command.

"To assimilate the Most High." Janno answered.

CHAPTER TWENTY SIX
SECTION SIX: MISSION CONTROL

"Blue Gemini to Mission Control, come in Mission Control" said the Voice.

"This is Mission Control" Luna answered.

"Activate magnetic beam" said the Voice.

"Magnetic beam activated" Luna responded, "What happens now, Father?"

"If all works out Ok," he said, "We'll be landing in two hours."

"We'll be waiting" Luna answered, "Mission Control, out!"

CHAPTER TWENTY SIX
SECTION SEVEN
TO SQUABBLE THE HIGH COMMAND

<Define the Most High?> questioned the High Command.

"He is an unlimited source of power." Janno described, "You have a sample source assimilated from Unit Sigma Five."

<Irrelevant: Code C element will engage in Squabble with Sentinels for evaluation and assimilation. Abilities will increase probabilities for assimilation of the Most High>

"Fair enough" Janno eluded aware that the High Command was trying to credit itself for the proposed idea. "I request to choose my own team."

<Request granted> spoke the High Command. The rest of the boys had reached the Squabble Den, the area where the players were kept. Now it was allowed that a Clip choose whomever he so wishes to be on his team and though it may have seemed that Janno could have chosen from Rex, Lyman, Ruffer, Allen, or Gormely to make up for the Medium the boys were missing but it was not strategically sound.

The members of the Lost Boys were not verse in the Warrior team's strategies.

"What are we going to do?" Arco asked.

"We're short one Medium" Orge agreed

"Astian?" Janno called out, "You've grown quite a bit during this adventure of ours. You're going to have to play Medium. You'll alternate with Arlos. Yuan will sub for me when I need a break."

"Can we do this?" Arco questioned, "Can we beat the High Command?"

"They're not so tough!" Astian motivated, "Remember our first fight with the Sentinel? We took him out! And we did it without wearing any armor to enhance our strength."

"We have a chance" Janno agreed, "Suit up." The warrior team donned their protective gear. They strapped their boots. They secured their pads. They arrayed themselves in Sentinel gear modified by Jeppe and Luna for their use. Janno walked to the center of the game floor. He positioned himself in a three stance position. "Warrior Unit Eighteen!" He called out, "Install positions!"

"In effect!" called out the team.

The High Command's Central Core Chamber's Digit One approached the center of the game floor and faced Janno head to head. Two black armored Sentinels positioned themselves to face Peff and Astian as the Medium guards. Then Arco and Orge couldn't help but feel a chill rise up their spines as two red armored Sentinels positioned themselves opposite the two Strongs. Arco and Orge glanced at each other. "Big deal!" Arco said.

<Alpha Unit One!> said the Digit One, <Install positions!> Then the disc came up from the center floor and the game was on.

"Side Sweep: to the Right!" Janno ordered, "Move!" Janno swept his right foot across the opposing Sentinels feet. He depressed the blue button in his left hand. This caused the magnetic field to envelope Janno's suit and with calibration Janno focused it upon his boot causing the Sentinel to be repulse onto the floor.   Janno had the disc.

He sprinted to the left while his Mediums made a right frontal assault.   Janno flung the disc to Astian and it made his name sake's sound, "Jnnnhhh!"   Astian caught hold of it and flung it back to Peff who sent it in an angled direction back to Janno who positioned himself at the slot and he then was able to make the deposit.

<Score One: Warrior Unit 18> called out the announcer, <Eight Bouts remaining: Warrior Unit 18 in Offense Status. Game: in effect!>

"Warriors, install positions!" Janno called out as the disc came out from beneath the center of the game floor, "Side Sweep to the Left, Move!" They performed the same maneuver only this time they had executed it to the opposite side.

<Score Two: Warrior Unit 18> called out the announcer, <Seven Bouts remaining: Warrior Unit 18 in Offense Status. Game status: in effect!>

"Warriors, install positions!" Janno called out as the disc came out from beneath the center of the game floor, "Sling Shot Thrust, Move!" Janno took the disc and retreated to his side of the game floor. The Mediums and the Strongs formed a "V" neck barrier at the center. Janno then charged forward. The Mediums took hold of his arms and launched him forward behind the defending Strongs. He bounced off their shoulders and flipped forward making the slot deposit.

<Score Three: Warrior Unit 18> called out the announcer, <Six Bouts remaining: Warrior Unit 18 in Offense Status: Game status: in effect!>

"I can't believe this is that easy" Arco commented.

"These guys aren't so tough." Astian added.

"Don't underestimate them" Janno spoke, "The only reason we're winning is because we're not giving the computers a chance to analyze our moves. Warriors, install positions." Janno was right. The High Command had not finished making its asses of the information analyzed during the first period. Janno did not know how long he had before the computers would counter act. Little did he know, the moves were all ready reaching the

Sentinels'   communication frequency.

<Alpha Unit One!> voiced the Digit One, <Install positions! Defense mode: The Wall, in effect!> Janno was taken by surprise. He had never heard any other team besides his announce the Wall in Defense mode. That distracted him long enough for the Digit One to land a punch into his face shield that sent him flying back into his side of the game floor. The Sentinels had possession of the disc. They strode forth.

"We gotta stop them!" Orge announced "Peff? Janno is down. You gotta call the shots!"

"Dosey doh's into the abdomen" Peff called out. Each Strong took hold of a Medium and spun him around. Each Medium came out of the spin with a leg poised to strike at the Sentinels' mid section. They activated the stasis field in their armor and the Sentinels were repelled, but it was futile. The opposing Clip had made the slot deposit. Janno was hurt. He called for time out.

<Slot Deposit!> called the announcer, < High Command Team Alpha One: in Offense Status. Game status: Break!>

"Janno, are you Ok?" Orge asked, "Can you continue?" {Can you continue?}, rung in his ears. He remembered that it was not so long ago when his coach had spoken those same words. He removed his helmet.

"My nose is bleeding!" he said, "I need a Medic. Yuan? Take my place." Yuan's heart jumped. He shoved his head into his helmet and took a position at the center of the game floor while Janno had his nose examined.

"Warriors!" Yuan called out, "Install positions! Wall Patrol, in effect!"

<Alpha Unit One!> called out the Digit One, <Virgin Ice, Move!> The disc hovered at the center of the game floor as the Warriors and the Sentinels battled to possess it. Janno with a swab inserted in his nose, once again was taken aback by the strategic call of the Sentinels.

{Impossible!} He thought, {No one should know those maneuvers. I created them and I told no one, much less, put them into play. Could the High Command have assimilated them from me? No. That wouldn't be right. It was the Counselor that was drained from me.}

<Score One: High Command Unit Alpha One> called out the announcer, <Five Bouts remaining: Unit Alpha One in Offense Status: Game status: in effect!> What was happening?

"Ouch!" Janno exclaimed as the swab swished inside his nose. Then without warning:

<Alert! Alert! MDV Virus: in Vicinity. Shut down communication links to High Command Central Core Chambers>

"That's going to be a little bit hard to do" Lyman commented, "We made the connection permanent. Yuan was glowing. His molecular frequency caused a domino effect, igniting Peff and Janno. All three began to glow. Janno's nose immediately healed.

<Alert! Alert! MDV Virus in effect. Initiate full High Command frequency communication link to override virus contamination>

"That's our cue fellas" Rex called out. They shot into the swarm of Sentinels that lied dormant in their cylinders.

<Alert! Alert! Sentinels in threat status: Override activation codes: Sentinels: Activate!>

"Let's get out of here!" Janno called out. The Lost Boys and the Warriors made their escape via the passage way built into all society units of the System. The High Command would not have its quarry escape. It launched a full scale hunt for the boys who wasted no time mounting an SPC and driving back to base camp.

"I hope this works" Rex said to Janno, "You did say you were the bait."

"Whatever happens," Arco spoke, "I just want you to know that it has been a pleasure engaging in this adventure with you all."

"This isn't the end" Astian complained, "It can't be. We've done what others only dreamt of."

"Well, we didn't actually win the game," Yuan said as a laser bolt struck the carrier up top.

CHAPTER TWENTY SIX
SECTION EIGHT: THE RETURN

"Mission Control, this is Blue Gemini, come in over!" said the Voice.

"Blue Gemini this is Mission Control, come in!" Luna answered.

"Activate landing procedures, we're coming down!" said the Voice.

At a distance the SPC neared the rebel base. The descending space capsule Luna and Jeppe were guiding, landed perfectly onto the three dimensional trapezoid-like platform they had built. The door slid open and the icy mist flowed from within. A figure stepped out.

<Alert! Alert!> said the approaching Sentinels in SPC's in direct communication link with the High Command, <MDV virus originating source in visual contact>

<Launch magnetic waves!> said the High Command in an attempt to drain the power of the figure that came out of the capsule. The link was made and

the figure pulled out an orb he held before him.

<Alert! Alert! High Command frequency: draining! Alert! Alert!> cried the High Command Central Core Chambers.

"That's enough out of you!" said the Voice as it drained all power from the High Command into a small orb, "And now we just simply turn you off!" All Sentinels throughout the system shut down as well as every Initialized personnel. For a moment everything was quite. Then:

"Counselor!" Janno exclaimed dropping to one knee.

"Excuse me, Sir?" Rex asked, "All these years the High Command has been seen as the most powerful entity in existence and you snuff it out in a mili second, who are you?"

"I am Adam" said the figure, "I am your Father."

TO BE CONCLUDED IN

THUNDER STORM: BOOK III

CPSIA information can be obtained
at www.ICGtesting.com
Printed in the USA
BVHW041435110719
553202BV00011B/492/P